The GHOST NEXT DOOR

ATTACK of the GRAVEYARD GHOULS

A SHOCKER on SHOCK STREET

LET'S GET INVISIBLE

The HAUNTED CAR

The ABOMINABLE SNOWMAN OF PASADENA

The BLOB THAT ATE EVERYONE

IT CAME FROM OHIO: MY LIFE AS A WRITER

Goosebumps®

MOST WANTED

PLANET of the LAWN GNOMES

SON of SLAPPY

Scholastic Children's Books
An imprint of Scholastic Ltd
Euston House, 24 Eversholt Street, London, NW1 1DB, UK
Registered office: Westfield Road, Southam, Warwickshire, CV47 0RA
SCHOLASTIC, GOOSEBUMPS, GOOSEBUMPS HORRORLAND
and associated logos are trademarks and/or registered trademarks of Scholastic
Inc.

First Published in the US by Scholastic Inc, 2013
First published in the UK by Scholastic Ltd, 2017

ISBN 978 1407 17886 8

Goosebumps books created by Parachute Press, Inc.

A CIP catalogue record for this book
is available from the British Library.

Printed by CPI Group (UK) Ltd, Croydon, CR0 4YY
Papers used by Scholastic Children's Books are made
from wood grown in sustainable forests.

1 3 5 7 9 10 8 6 4 2

www.scholastic.co.uk

Goosebumps®

HOW I MET MY MONSTER

R.L. STINE

SCHOLASTIC

WELCOME. YOU ARE MOST WANTED.

Come in. I'm R.L. Stine. Welcome to the Goosebumps office.

Please excuse the mess. My housecreeper didn't show up today because she's sick. Uh-oh. That's not a lumpy rug you're standing on. She was sick all over the floor.

Please sit down. You can clean your shoes off later.

We had a monster party here last night. It was a surprise good-bye party for my friend Oggie. Oggie didn't know he was going away. But at the end of the party, one of the guests ATE him.

That's why it was a surprise good-bye party.

I see you are admiring the WANTED posters on the wall. Those posters show the creepiest, crawliest, grossest monsters and bad dudes of all time. They are the MOST WANTED characters from the Goosebumps books.

I am telling their stories in the Goosebumps: Most Wanted series.

You're not afraid of monsters, are you? Well, what if there was a monster in your class at school? What if you were the only one who knew he was a monster? And what if he decided *you* were his next victim?

Then would you be a tiny bit afraid?

Well, here's a boy named Noah Bienstock. The kids all call him Bean. He has a story to tell you about monsters.

Better read it carefully. You never know when someone might be planning a surprise good-bye party for *you*!

After you read Bean's story, you will definitely know why the monster in his class is MOST WANTED.

Have you ever felt so frightened, you couldn't breathe? Like your whole body just locked in fear, and you couldn't even blink your eyes?

That's how I feel right now. I can't move and I can't think straight.

My name is Noah Bienstock and I'm twelve. Everyone calls me Bean, even my parents.

I'm underwater. Deep underwater. And it's cold down here. It feels like icicles brushing against my skin. Each ripple of the soupy green water makes me shiver.

I know I have to move. Because something is coming after me. Something dark and big.

I see only a billowing black shadow in the water. Like an inkblot. Moving fast, in a straight line. It starts to take shape. It's some sort of creature.

Ohh. I've seen it before. It's the monster.

I pull my arms forward and try to swim. My muscles don't want to work. The water suddenly

1

feels heavy, as if it's pushing down on me, trying to sink me.

The shadow rolls over me, covering me in its darkness, making the water even colder.

I shudder. My whole body prickles from the cold. I want to scream. Scream for help. But I'm deep underwater.

No one can scream underwater. Even in a dream.

Yes, I know I'm dreaming. I've had this dream before.

I know it's a dream, but I can't stop my terror. Each time, the dream seems as real as my life. Each time, the monster behind the inky black shadow comes closer . . . closer to swallowing me up.

I ignore my pounding heartbeats and force myself to swim. I kick hard. My hands churn the water. Faster. Harder. But I can't pull myself out of the cold shadow. It reaches over me with tentacles like some kind of octopus.

I can't escape. It's too fast, too big. The shadow spreads over me, making me shudder again as I frantically churn the water. I know the monster is close behind it.

I'm dreaming. I'm dreaming about the monster again. But I can't wake up. I can't raise myself from the green-black ocean depths.

The water bubbles and swirls. Long weeds

slap at my face and wrap around my arms. *Let me go. Let me go.*

My chest is bursting. I need to breathe. I need to scream.

And then I hear a growled whisper, carried by a strong underwater wave. A terrifying low voice, calling to me: *I'll find you. You can't hide. I promise I'll find you.*

My terror makes my arms stronger. I slap at the water. Push through the long, sharp weeds. Swim up. Yes. My thudding heartbeats are like an engine. I kick and thrash my arms and reach the surface.

Yes!

My head shoots up over the water. I struggle to suck in a deep breath.

But I feel the monster beneath me. I feel it wrap its powerful arms around my legs. And pull me hard . . . pull me down.

I can't kick free. I can't swim. I can't breathe. I can't escape.

Down . . . Down . . .

Wake up! Why can't I WAKE UP?

"I had the dream again," I said.

Mom poured a pile of Wheaties into my bowl. She shook her head and tsk-tsked. "Again?" She tilted the milk carton over the cereal.

"I can pour my own milk," I said. "I'm not a baby."

"I like to pour it," she said. "Makes me feel like a real mom, you know. Like in the TV commercials."

Mom and Dad aren't like TV parents. Mom is a rocket scientist. Really. She's always flying off to some desert to work on a new kind of space rocket. Dad manages a pet shop at the mall. He's always bringing strange birds home to show off to me.

"Why do I have to have nonfat milk?" I grumbled. "It tastes like water. Why can't I have *real* milk?"

She squinted at me. "Because you're a chub?"

"I'm *not* a chub." I slammed my spoon on the tabletop. "I'm not even the biggest kid in my class. Not even close. Why do you always have to say I'm a chub?"

"Sorry," she said. "Look. Don't take it out on me. Okay? You're upset because of the dream."

"Yeah. Why do I have so many horrible nightmares about being chased by monsters? You're a scientist. Tell me, why do I keep having this underwater dream?"

Mom dropped into the chair across the table and took a long sip of coffee. "Because you're nervous."

"Huh? Nervous about drowning?"

"No, Bean. You're nervous about the swim team tryouts. You're not sure you're good enough to make the team. So you keep having nightmares about swimming."

I stared hard at her. "Maybe you're right."

"Of course I'm right. I'm a scientist."

"But . . . why do the dreams seem so *real*?"

She took another sip of coffee. It must have been really hot. The heat made her glasses steam up. "Because you have a really powerful imagination, I guess."

I liked that answer. I *do* have a good imagination. I think it's because I spend a lot of time by myself, thinking up things.

I don't have a ton of friends. I don't talk a lot in school, and it's hard for me to hang out with other kids. I can never think of anything to say.

5

I think it's because I'm kind of shy. And that makes life a little tough. And a little lonely.

My best friend is Lissa Gardener. She's in my class, and she lives upstairs from me at Sternom House, our apartment building.

Lissa and I look like we come from different planets. I'm short and a little chubby. I have curly black hair and dark eyes and wear glasses like my mom and dad. Lissa is tall and thin, with straight blond hair and blue eyes.

She is trying out for the girls' swim team. But she doesn't have nightmares about it because she knows she's really good at sports. She has other friends, too. But since we live in the same apartment building, we end up spending a lot of time together.

I went to my room and got dressed for school. I expected to find puddles of water on my floor. You know. From my dream.

Bright sunlight filled my bedroom window. But I still saw that terrifying shadow, the shadow of the monster rolling over me deep under the water.

I shivered. I couldn't shake the dream from my mind.

I knew Mom was right. I was just stressed about the swim team tryouts.

I didn't really want to try out. But Lissa said I had to get into some activities at school. She said it would help me make more friends.

I shouted good-bye to Mom. Then I swung my backpack onto my shoulders and headed out the door.

We live on the fourth floor. I never take the elevator. I always go down the stairs. My sneakers clanged on the metal steps as I ran down, my hand sliding down the narrow railing.

I pushed open the door and stepped outside. It was a sunny spring day with puffy white clouds high overhead. The air was warm and smelled of flowers.

I stopped when I saw a red-and-white moving van parked at the curb. A family was watching as movers started to unload their furniture and cartons from the back of the big truck.

A new family moving into the building.

I saw three kids. Two of them were little. But one could be about my age. He turned as I started to walk past. He had brown hair down over his forehead to his eyes. He didn't smile. He turned back to the truck before I could say hi or anything.

Sternom House is very big. Families move in and out of our building all the time. But I always hoped a boy my age would move in and we could be friends.

I heard a heavy thud as one of the workers dropped a carton off the truck. I didn't wait to see what happened next. I turned the corner and trotted down Elm toward school.

7

I was halfway down the block, past another apartment house and then a row of little houses. I heard footsteps. Coming on fast.

I didn't have time to turn around. Icy fingers wrapped around the back of my neck.

I screamed. I couldn't help myself. Suddenly, I was back in my dream.

3

I let out another shriek.

The fingers loosened on my neck. I heard a giggle.

I turned and found Lissa behind me. She had a grin on her face, as if she'd won some kind of game. Her blue eyes flashed in the sunlight.

I don't know what her problem is. She's supposed to be my friend. Why does she like to scare me?

"Why'd you do that?" I snapped, rubbing the back of my neck.

She shrugged. "Just felt like it." That made her giggle again. "Bean, why are you so jumpy?"

"I don't know." I shifted my backpack and started walking again. A big SUV rumbled past and some kids shouted at us out the window. "I guess it's because I had another bad dream."

"Another monster dream?"

"I can't seem to shake it off," I said.

She pulled up a blade of grass and put it between her lips. I don't know why she likes to do that. "What happened in the dream?"

"Some kind of monster chased me. I couldn't see it clearly. I was underwater and there was this big shadow in the water. But I knew it was there, and I knew it was chasing me."

She shoved my shoulder and I stumbled off the sidewalk. "Why didn't you chase it back? You're a big dude. Maybe it would be afraid of you."

"Don't you get it?" I said. "It was a *monster*. Something big and ugly and dangerous. It wanted to kill me. It wanted to drown me. It wasn't funny, Lissa. So stop laughing at me. It . . . it was so real."

She rolled her eyes. "Sor-ry. I didn't think it was funny. I just thought —"

We crossed the street. Our school came into view in the next block. "Do *you* believe in monsters?" I asked.

"Of *course* I do," she said. "Doesn't everyone?" She pointed. "Here comes one now."

I groaned when I saw the big guy hurrying toward us. Harlan Egman. A huge, hulking bear who lives in a house close to the school.

How do you spell Harlan? D-I-S-A-S-T-E-R.

It was too late to run. Harlan's big shoes stomped the grass as he ran at us like a charging bull.

"He's always chasing after me," I murmured to Lissa. "Maybe *he's* the monster in my dream."

Before Lissa could reply, Harlan ran right into me, bumping me hard with his big belly, knocking me to the grass onto my butt.

He laughed. "Oops. Couldn't stop." He reached out both hands to help pull me back to my feet. But when I was halfway up, he let go, and I fell back down again.

"You're a klutz, Bean," Harlan barked. He turned to Lissa, like he expected her to give him trouble.

But she didn't say a word. Just stared down at me, flat on my back on top of my backpack. I climbed slowly to my feet. I didn't think any bones were broken. That's a *win* when Harlan is around.

He moved up close to me, so close he was stepping on my toes. "How you doing, Bean?" His breath smelled of coffee. The kid drinks *coffee* in the morning!

"I was doing okay till you showed up," I muttered.

He laughed as if I'd made a really good joke. Then his smile faded, and his big black eyes narrowed at me. "Did your mom give you lunch money?"

My heart started to do flip-flops. "Yeah," I said.

"She meant to give it to *me*," Harlan said. He stuck out his hand. "Hand it over."

I took a deep breath. "Harlan, I'm so totally hungry at lunchtime every day because of you."

He waved his big paw in my face. "Give me the money, and I won't ask again until *tomorrow* morning."

"Ha-ha," I muttered. "Funny."

Finally, Lissa spoke up. "Stop picking on Bean," she told Harlan.

His grin spread over his meaty face. "Okay. I'll pick on *you*." He wrapped his huge hand around her face and gave her a hard push. She staggered back into a tree.

"Hey!" I cried. "Why'd you do that?"

"Because I like to shove?" He lowered his shoulder, darted forward, and rammed into my stomach.

I doubled over. Dropped to the ground. Into a deep mud puddle.

"I hate violence — don't you?" Harlan growled.

I could feel the wet mud seep through my jeans.

Lissa and I handed over our lunch money. Harlan ran off toward school, crowing like a rooster at the top of his lungs.

"Another awesome day," I muttered.

Lissa helped pull me to my feet. "You're almost as heavy as Harlan, Bean. Why don't you ever stand up to him?"

"Because I'd like to keep my head facing the right way," I said. I wiped a mud smear from my glasses. Then I tried to brush the mud off my jeans, but it was soaked in.

Lissa straightened the backpack on my shoulders. "Maybe if you stand up to Harlan, your monster dreams will go away," she said.

"For sure," I said. "And maybe I'll sprout wings this afternoon and fly to the moon."

We walked the rest of the way to school in silence. There wasn't anything left to say.

I had a lot of grim thoughts. I mean, my dreams were frightening. And my walk to school every morning was frightening, too. Let's face facts. My life was pretty scary.

And soon it would get a lot scarier.

I was about to meet my monster.

I got to school and dropped some books in my locker. I heard a couple of girls laughing across the hall, and I knew they were laughing about the huge, wet mud stain on my jeans.

I thought about hiding in my locker till school was over. I really did. I mean, could it be any more embarrassing than to have the whole back of your jeans covered in a big brown stain?

I made my way to Mrs. Fielding's room, walking sideways. I tried to keep my back against the wall so no one could see the stain.

I edged into the classroom and crab-walked to my seat near the back of the room. Lissa sat in the front. She stared at me the whole time. Couldn't she figure out why I had to walk this way?

Finally, I dropped into my chair. I was breathing hard, and sweat poured down my cheeks and forehead. This day *had* to get better — right?

Mrs. Fielding stepped into the room. She is young and awesomely pretty and wears jeans and T-shirts just like the kids. Everyone wants to be in her class because she's so totally cool.

She was followed by a kid I'd never seen in school before. He had a helmet of brown hair on his head, a pointed nose, and eyes close together so he looked kind of like a bird. He wore a red soccer jersey with the number 00 in white on the front, and faded cargo jeans.

"We have to welcome a new student today," Mrs. Fielding said, smiling, with her hand on the kid's shoulder.

Why did he look familiar?

I leaned forward and squinted hard at the kid. He was pale and looked very nervous. His little eyes darted from side to side.

I've seen him before, I thought. *I know I have.*

"This is Monroe Morton," Mrs. Fielding announced. "Tell us where you come from, Monroe."

He shrugged. "I come from a lot of places," he said. He had a low, growly voice. He spoke slowly, like he was thinking hard about the answer. "My family . . . we move around a lot."

"Well, welcome to Franklin Pierce Middle School," Mrs. Fielding said. "I'm sure everyone in class will help you feel at home here." She pointed to the empty seat next to me. "You can take that desk next to Noah."

She's the only person in the world who doesn't call me Bean.

Monroe made his way toward the desk. He had a funny, shuffling walk. He slid into the seat next to mine and dropped his backpack on the floor.

Why does he look familiar? I asked myself again.

He grinned at me. His two front teeth were crooked and stuck out like Bugs Bunny teeth. He brushed back his dark hair. "Hey, we have the same backpack."

I glanced down at my backpack at my feet. "Yeah. Guess so."

"I had to search all over for mine," he said in his growly voice. "Everything is messed up at my place. We just moved into our new apartment this morning."

That's where I saw him!

"You moved into Sternom House this morning?" I said.

He nodded.

"I live there, too," I said. "I'm Noah Bienstock. Everyone calls me Bean. I saw you and your family this morning."

"Hey, yeah? We're neighbors?"

Mrs. Fielding told everyone to take out a pencil and some paper. I leaned down and opened my backpack.

"We move around a lot," Monroe said. "It's way tough. New school . . . new friends. You know. Hey, maybe you can show me where the lunchroom is later."

"Yeah. No problem," I said.

That reminded me that I didn't have any lunch money. I glanced down the row of desks and saw Harlan. He had a huge grin on his face. I don't know why. He was drumming his pencil on his desk and tapping his big feet, annoying everyone around him.

My stomach growled. I was hungry already. It was going to be a long day. I started to write my name at the top of the paper.

"Wow. You're left-handed," Monroe said. "Me too!" He bumped knuckles with me.

I liked this guy. He seemed really friendly.

I'd been thinking about how I needed to get over my shyness and make new friends. Maybe Monroe was the friend I needed.

When the lunch bell rang, we stashed our backpacks in our lockers. Then I led him downstairs to the lunchroom. He carried an enormous brown lunch bag in one hand. It was almost as big as a shopping bag!

The room was crowded and noisy as always. Some kids were tossing apples across the tables at each other. One boy got hit in the head. He let out a scream, and the apple war quickly stopped.

I saw Harlan in the cafeteria line. His tray was stacked high with pizza slices. He was having a great lunch with the lunch money he took from Lissa and me. Harlan shoved the girl ahead of him in line, just because he likes to shove.

17

I led Monroe to the table in back where I usually ate. We sat down across from each other. Monroe started to pull out sandwiches and cheese sticks and fruit snacks and other stuff from his giant lunch bag.

He slid a sandwich over to me, and a carton of juice.

"Thanks," I said. "I had lunch money, but . . ."

I saw Harlan at the next table. He had pizza sauce all over his fat face. He opened his mouth and let out a disgusting, loud burp. Everyone at his table laughed.

Lissa stepped up to my table. She nodded to Monroe, then she turned to me. "Roz Hoff loaned me some money. Want to share my lunch?"

"That's okay," I said. "Monroe is sharing his lunch with me."

Monroe flashed Lissa a grin. He had chunks of tuna fish stuck to his teeth.

"Later," Lissa said. She trotted toward the cafeteria line.

I turned back to Monroe. He had a sandwich in each hand. He was stuffing them into his mouth, wolfing them down one after the other. He was almost swallowing them whole! He barely chewed them.

After a while, he saw me staring at him. "My mom always packs a humongous lunch," he said. "I have a MONSTER appetite."

5

Swim team tryouts were Friday after school. Monroe asked if he could come to the pool and watch. He said he could cheer me on.

We'd been hanging out together all week. We were getting to be pretty good friends. I told him how tense I was about trying out. But I didn't tell him about my nightmares.

I guess I didn't think I knew him well enough. I didn't want him to think I was weird. Or maybe I didn't want him to laugh at me when I said I dreamed about a monster pulling me under the water.

But as Monroe and I stepped into the school swimming pool, I couldn't force the horrible dream from my mind.

My school is very lucky. We have an Olympic-size pool. It's behind the main building. The walls are blue tile and the ceiling is a giant sky-light. There are locker rooms at one end and bleachers on the sides for people to watch the swim meets.

I took a deep breath. I love the smell of chlorine. Sunlight beamed down over the sparkling blue water. The air felt hot and steamy and made my face prickle.

A few kids were already in the pool. They were doing warm-up exercises.

Coach Waller is a huge dude. Really. He always reminds me of a light-haired version of the Hulk. He looks like he should be a wrestling coach. But he teaches math and coaches swimming and tennis.

He came lumbering over to me as I stepped toward the locker room. "Bean, get changed. The pool is going to be crowded. Someone messed up the schedule. So we're having boys' team and girls' team tryouts at the same time. We'll swim the width of the pool instead of the length."

"This is my friend Monroe," I said. "He just came to watch."

Waller eyed Monroe. "You're the new kid, right? You don't swim?"

Monroe shrugged. "Not very well."

Waller pointed to the bleachers across the pool. "Go have a seat, Monroe. Bean, get moving. I want to see what you've got. I'm not looking for speed today. Just endurance."

Endurance?

Did that mean he wanted to see how many laps I could swim?

I felt a tremor of fear. My stomach did a slow flip-flop. My dad taught me to swim. He says I've got a really good stroke. But maybe he was just being nice. Maybe I'm not as good as the other guys. Maybe my swimming is totally lame.

Waller hurried off to talk to some other swimmers. I gazed into the water. Ripples of sunlight made the whole pool seem to be rolling, as if it had waves.

I saw Lissa in the deep end. She was warming up by swimming slow laps across the width of the pool. I waved to her, but I don't think she saw me.

Lissa, you got me into this. I hope it isn't a total disaster.

As I stepped into the locker room to change, my nightmare flashed back into my mind. I saw the monster's dark shadow in the water, sliding toward me. And once again, I pictured the monster deep under the water, pulling me down . . . down.

"No!"

I didn't realize I had screamed out loud. A couple of guys turned from their lockers to stare at me. I could feel myself blushing.

At the far end of the room, I saw Harlan. He had a white towel in his hand, and he was snapping it against the back of a small, red-haired kid. The kid was begging Harlan to stop. Harlan just laughed and snapped him again.

Back out at the pool, I did some stretching exercises. The pool was filling up with swimmers. Voices rang loudly off the tile walls. At one side of the pool, two boys were having a splashing contest. Coach Waller quickly broke it up and told the boys to start practicing their breast stroke.

He motioned to me. "Bean, go out to the deep end and do some slow laps to warm up. Practice your underwater turns off the wall, okay? I'm going to test you first."

I nodded. My stomach flip-flopped again. Why did I have to go first?

I lowered myself into the water. It was warmer than I expected. They keep the pool heated pretty high. I floated away from the pool wall.

Lissa was still doing her practice laps near the deep end. She glided easily with slow, steady strokes. I wished I could be as calm as she was.

I looked for Monroe in the bleachers. I couldn't find him. Maybe he got bored and changed his mind about watching.

I ducked my head under the water. Then I edged between a group of girls and started to swim toward the deep end. I heard some guys laughing. Their laughter echoed off the walls. A whistle blew. The pool grew quieter.

I began to swim. I felt pretty strong. I kept my head down and tried to keep my stroke steady. I did a lap across the pool, then a lap back.

My heart beat faster. I raised my swim goggles and searched for Lissa. But she wasn't there. She must have finished her warm-up.

I decided to do a few more laps. Moving through the water so easily was helping me get rid of my fear. I was suddenly glad to be tested first. I felt strong and confident.

I swam a few more strokes, kicking hard. And then a feeling of dread in the pit of my stomach made me stop.

Something down there. Something under the water.

It wasn't a hunch. I *knew* it.

I knew there was something dark and ugly down below.

I bobbed on the surface, breathing hard. My arms . . . my legs . . . they froze.

Water splashed my face. I struggled to slow my racing heart.

Not my imagination . . . I'm not dreaming this. . . .

I had to look down. I had to see it. I had to prove to myself that I wasn't crazy. My fear was real — because the creature in the water was real.

I lowered my head and peered down into the blue-green ripples of water.

Yes! I saw something move. A flash of black.

A shadow sliding through the water. Gliding like a huge manta ray. Like a winged bat. A big dark blot deep in the water ... moving forward rapidly ... coming for me.

The monster was coming for me. Ready to grab me and pull me down.

I saw it. I saw its inky shadow.

My nightmare has come true!

Gasping, shivering, I raised my head. And my shrill scream of terror echoed off the high pool walls.

It grabbed me.

I felt its cold tentacle as it wrapped around my neck.

My scream cut off. My breath cut off.

I tugged hard. Blindly, I struggled to free myself from its grasp.

But it was stronger than me. It tightened around my neck and started to pull me.

I thrashed the water. Tried to kick at it. But I was helpless in its grasp.

And then I heard its voice in my ear: "Dude — stop fighting me."

Huh?

I turned my head — and saw Harlan. Harlan had his arm around my shoulder. He was pulling me toward the shallow end.

"Stop fighting me, you jerk!" he cried. "I'm rescuing you. What's your problem?"

My body went limp. I let out a long whoosh of

air. I could see kids watching, alarmed looks on their faces, as Harlan dragged me across the pool. A group of girls huddled together, pointing at me, all talking at once.

I knew my life was ruined. I was doomed. Totally doomed.

From now on, people would talk about my panic attack. For the rest of my life, people would see me and remember how I had screamed like a baby in the school swimming pool. How I froze in terror and had to be pulled to safety by the worst person in the world — Harlan Egman.

"Just kill me now," I told Harlan. "Please. Let me drown right here. I'm begging you."

He unwrapped his arm from my shoulders and helped me stand in the shallow end. "Hey, I just saved your life, moron!" He slapped me hard on the shoulder. "Do you know why?"

"Because you believe human life is sacred?"

That made him roar with laughter. "No. Because now you'll be buying me lunch *forever*!"

He laughed again and pushed me up the ladder and out of the pool. I stood dripping on the pool edge. Everyone still stared.

Coach Waller came rumbling toward me. "Bean? What was *that* all about?" he demanded.

Before I could answer, Harlan came up behind me. He grabbed the sides of my swim trunks in both hands — and tugged them down to my ankles!

Will I ever forget the sound of the screams and the laughter as I stood there totally naked?

What's your guess?

7

Somehow I survived the rest of the day. At dinner, when Mom and Dad asked how the swim team tryout went, I lowered my head and mumbled into my mashed potatoes.

"Can't hear you, Bean," Dad said.

I mumbled again.

"Guess it didn't go well," Mom said.

"Guess it didn't," I said. I could feel myself blushing again. I started to blush every time I thought about standing there in front of everyone with my swim trunks down at my ankles.

Monday morning, I met Monroe outside our building, and we walked to school. Monroe talked about the science assignment.

At the end of the block, I stopped. "Did you see what Harlan did to me at the pool on Friday?" I said.

Monroe shook his head. "No. I had to leave."

I squinted at him. "You had to leave?"

"I got a text from my mom, and I had to go home. What happened at the pool? Did you make the team?"

"I made the Embarrassed-For-Life team," I told him. I explained what happened.

"Wow," Monroe said. "Wow."

"After I pulled my trunks up, Coach Waller asked me to stay and try out," I said. "But I couldn't. I just wanted to get out of there as fast as I could."

Monroe groaned. "Did the coach punish Harlan?"

"No. Waller had his back turned. He didn't see Harlan do it." I sighed. "I really thought I saw a shadow moving in the water. It wasn't just a panic attack. I've got monsters on the brain. I have to find a way to get over it."

We crossed the street. Two girls on bikes rolled by. They started to laugh. I wondered if they were laughing about me.

"This guy Harlan is a bad dude," Monroe said.

"Yes. He is a —" I stopped. I saw the big jerk thundering across a lawn, waving to us. "Oh, no. Here he comes."

We stopped and watched him. His backpack flapped on his back. His big shoes thudded loudly on the ground.

I grabbed Monroe's arm. "Listen. Do whatever he says. Really. Don't argue with him or try to fight him. I'm serious. He really will hurt you."

Monroe pulled away from me. "Forget that," he said in a low voice. "You hold his arms — and I'll bite his throat."

I gasped. "Huh? *What* did you say?"

"Just kidding," Monroe whispered. His hair had fallen over his eyes. He brushed it back. He had a strange expression on his face. I couldn't tell if it was anger — or fear. "It was a joke, Bean."

"Well, don't joke with Harlan," I warned. "He doesn't get jokes. Be careful. Do whatever he says."

Harlan bumped up against me, breathing hard. I stumbled back a few steps. He had big drops of sweat rolling down his forehead. His eyes slid from me to Monroe.

"Hey, new kid," he snarled at Monroe. "Think you're tough?"

"No," Monroe answered softly.

Harlan snapped his fingers over Monroe's nose. "Think you're tough as me?"

"No," Monroe replied. His nose turned bright red. "I don't think I'm tough."

"Did Beany Boy tell you how I de-pantsed him yesterday?"

Monroe nodded. "Yes. He told me."

Harlan snapped Monroe's nose again.

"Oww." Monroe rubbed his sore nose.

"That's a big lunch bag you got there," Harlan said. He squeezed Monroe's lunch with a big paw.

"Yeah, kinda," Monroe said.

Harlan grinned. "Since you're a new kid, I'm gonna give you a break."

"A break?"

"Yeah. I'll let you give me your whole lunch."

Monroe's mouth dropped open. "That's a *break*?"

"Yeah," Harlan replied. "I know I'm too nice, but I can't help it. Hand it over." Harlan stuck out his hand, waiting for Monroe to give him the lunch bag.

But Monroe pulled back. He raised his eyes and stared hard at Harlan. Monroe's whole body tensed, and he gritted his teeth.

Oh, no. Please, no. What's he going to do? Monroe, please don't try to fight Harlan.

8

"Okay. Here," Monroe said. He stuck his lunch bag into Harlan's outstretched hand.

I let out a sigh of relief. I was sure Monroe was about to do something crazy. And fighting Harlan is *crazy*.

Harlan tossed the bag in the air and then caught it in both hands. Then he took his thumbs and smeared both lenses on my glasses. Then he spun away and ran off laughing. What a pig.

I turned back to Monroe. His face was bright red and he was panting like an animal. Both of his hands were balled into tight fists.

I put a hand on his shoulder. It was trembling. His whole body was trembling.

"Calm down," I said. "Take a breath. There is nothing we can do about Harlan."

Monroe's color slowly returned to normal. But he was still panting.

"He's a monster," I said. "He's giving me bad dreams. Really."

Monroe squinted at me. "You have nightmares about Harlan?"

"About a monster," I said. "I think the monster is Harlan. Lissa says if I ever stood up to Harlan, the dreams would stop. But . . . I'm too afraid."

A car horn honked as a black Volvo rolled by. Some kids waved at us from the backseat. We started walking again. It was a cloudy gray morning. The air felt damp and hot.

"I think I'll run ahead," Monroe said. "Sometimes it helps me calm down if I run."

Before I could reply, he took off. He leaned way forward and ran as if he were charging at something. He rocketed across the street without looking for traffic and kept going.

I trotted behind him. I didn't feel like running that hard. Halfway down the block, our school came into view.

Suddenly, the clouds parted and a beam of sunlight washed down, so surprising and bright, I had to shut my eyes.

Sunspots flashed before my eyelids. They faded quickly. Clouds covered the sun again.

I opened my eyes — and gasped. What was that *creature* running toward the school?

It was covered in brown fur. And even from this distance, I could see long, pointed teeth curling from its open mouth.

A monster! A real one.

My breath caught in my throat. I froze and stared as it lumbered across the school yard toward the entrance to the school.

Is that Monroe? Can it be Monroe?

The sun poured down again. I blinked. The monster had vanished.

No one there. No monster. No Monroe. I saw two boys riding their bikes around the side of the building. Other kids made their way up the front walk. A girl dropped her backpack and papers flew across the grass.

"I'm going totally crazy," I said out loud.

I decided it had to be the bright sunlight in my eyes. It made me imagine I saw a monster.

Monroe isn't a monster. What's WRONG with me?

My dad loves animals. He grew up on a farm where they had chickens and goats and sheep. He's always telling us stories about how he got in trouble trying to hide the animals in his bedroom at night when he was little.

I guess that's why he manages a pet shop. It's a cool little store at the mall called Pets & More Pets. It's mostly birds and fish. But he has hamsters and gerbils and guinea pigs, too, and sometimes some kittens.

On Saturday, Dad gave me a ride to the mall. Monroe and I planned to meet there and hang out. And I wanted to check out the store. I needed to choose an animal to bring to the school pet fair.

There would be $300 prizes for the strangest pets — and the most talented. I thought maybe I'd bring one of Dad's mynah birds. Or maybe some weirdo kind of fish.

How lucky was I to have a whole pet shop to choose from!

I always have to laugh when I ride with Dad. He drives a little Ford Focus, and he's so tall, he has to fold himself up to sit behind the wheel. His knees come up to the steering wheel and his head bumps the car roof. Mom says he needs a bigger car. But Dad says he's totally comfortable.

We drove past the school and made a left turn on Main Street. "How's school going?" Dad asked.

"Okay," I said.

He waited for me to say more, but I didn't.

"Too bad about the swim team thing," Dad said, eyes straight ahead on the road.

"Yeah," I said. "Too bad. But Coach Waller says I can try out again later."

That's not happening.

I could feel myself blushing, just thinking about standing there with my swimsuit down.

"So you have a new friend? This guy Monroe?" Dad said, signaling his turn into the mall.

"Yeah," I said. "He's a good guy. We're . . . a lot alike, I guess."

Again, I pictured the dark-furred monster loping toward the school in the bright sunlight. I couldn't get the picture out of my mind.

It had to be my imagination running wild again. I wish I would stop seeing monsters everywhere.

36

Dad parked in his reserved spot, and we walked into the mall. It was already crowded with Saturday morning shoppers. Dad took out his keys and unlocked the pet-shop door. A tall, red macaw watched us from the front window. It started to squawk, as if saying hello.

I told Dad I'd meet him later and hurried off to find Monroe. We'd made a plan to meet in front of the bakery called The Doughnut Hole. But I didn't see him there.

Something bumped me hard from behind. A jolt of fear ran down my body. But it was just a woman trying to carry packages and push a baby stroller. She apologized three or four times and moved on.

I gazed across the aisle and saw Lissa. She was walking with her mom, coming out of a dress store. "Hey!" I called to her, and she came jogging over. "Lissa, what's up?"

She made a face. "My cousin is getting married, and Mom dragged me here to find a dress to wear. Everything she picks out is, like, for a five-year-old. I said, 'Why can't I just get a new pair of jeans?'"

Lissa opened her mouth in a growl. "AAAAAGGGH. I hate shopping with her."

Mrs. Gardener waved for Lissa to come back into the store. "I'm coming!" Lissa shouted. She turned to me. "What are you doing here?"

"Meeting Monroe," I said. I glanced over to The Doughnut Hole. He still wasn't there.

I leaned closer to Lissa. "Can I tell you something? Something I saw?"

She squinted at me. "Let me guess. You saw another monster?"

I nodded. "Yes. I did."

She stared at me. "You're serious?"

"Lissa, I saw this big, furry creature. Really. Running across the school yard. I . . . I don't think I imagined it. I saw it so clearly. It had piles of dark fur and long yellow fangs."

Lissa squinted at me. "You're serious?" she repeated.

"Of *course* I'm serious." I didn't mean to sound so breathless. But I wanted her to believe me. "Monroe was running ahead of me. Then the sun came out and got in my eyes. And I saw a monster, furry, with teeth and —"

"Calm down, Bean." Lissa grabbed my shoulders. "Okay. You saw a monster. Deal with it."

"Huh? Deal with it?"

"Deal with it."

I didn't really know what she meant. We stared at each other for a long moment. "Want to hang out with Monroe and me?" I said finally.

"How can I?" She glanced across the aisle at her mother, impatiently tapping her foot in front of the clothing store. "Got to go. If you see any monsters, don't scream for me — okay?"

"Ha-ha," I said. "Is your middle name Lame? You are so not funny."

I saw Monroe walking toward the doughnut shop. I waved and ran over to him. He had a big bag of tortilla chips in one hand and was stuffing his face with them.

"One of my hungry days," he said. "My mom says it's probably a growth spurt."

"A growth spurt?"

He nodded, chewing loudly. "Yeah, you know. When you suddenly shoot up an inch or two?"

I sighed. "That never happened to me." I pictured the furry monster running in sunlight. Was that one of Monroe's growth spurts?

Stop being stupid, Bean.

We walked around for an hour or so. We bought soft pretzels with mustard, and then we bought cinnamon buns. We had a good time kidding around, joking about Harlan and other kids at school.

Suddenly, Monroe stopped and rubbed his stomach. "You hear that? My stomach is growling like an angry bear."

"And that means . . ."

"It means I'm *starving*. Come on, dude. Over here." He pulled me into The Burger Balloon. It's a huge hamburger place with red-and-blue balloons floating at the ceiling and balloons bobbing on the walls and over the booths.

We moved down the long aisle, searching for a table. I waved to Lissa and her mom. They had a booth near the window.

We sat down on the other side of the restaurant.

A tall waitress in a red-and-blue uniform took our order. Monroe ordered two cheeseburgers and two orders of fries. He really *was* hungry.

Across from us, a mother raised a big cup, giving her baby a milkshake through a straw. Two teenagers held hands across their table, waiting for their food to arrive.

"Why is it taking so long?" Monroe said, glancing around. He rubbed his stomach. "Hear that?"

I actually *did* hear it. His stomach growled so loud, it sounded like a lion's roar.

"Whoa." I stared at him. "Weird."

His face turned red. His stomach growled again. He tapped his hands on the table. "I am way hungry."

The waitress brought the food for the two teenagers. As she set down the tray, the aroma of the burgers floated over to us.

Monroe jumped to his feet.

"Where are you going?" I asked.

"Bathroom," he said. "Be right back."

I watched him stomp to the back of the restaurant. Two kids from my school sat down in a booth against the wall. I called to them, but they couldn't hear me over the voices and clatter and loud music.

I suddenly felt pretty hungry myself. I glanced around for our waitress.

I sat up straight when I heard a shrill scream. A scream from the kitchen.

"Help! A MONSTER! Somebody — *help*!"

I spun around and stared at the back. The double kitchen doors had small, round windows, but I couldn't see into the kitchen.

Did I hear right? Did the screaming woman say there was a *monster*?

"Help! Monster! Help!" The frightened screams again.

"See!" I wanted to shout to Lissa across the restaurant, but she and her mom had already left.

The restaurant grew silent, except for the blaring music. Some people jumped up. A few hurried toward the kitchen. A baby started to cry.

I leaped to my feet just as Monroe came walking back. He had his hands in his jeans pockets and walked slowly, calmly.

"Bean, what's up?" he asked. "I thought I heard screams. Did you hear them?"

I didn't answer. I was staring hard. Staring at the chunk of raw hamburger on Monroe's chin.

10

Monroe slid into the booth. "Still no food? Where is it?" he asked.

I stared hard at him. Two minutes ago, he said he was going to the bathroom. A few seconds later, the cook started screaming about a monster in the kitchen.

I worked up my courage. Took a deep breath. "Uh . . . Monroe . . ." I pointed to his chin. "What is that on your chin?"

Did you turn into a monster and grab raw hamburger meat in the kitchen?

Monroe reached up and tugged the chunk off his face. He examined it. "My bubblegum!" he said. He laughed. "I *wondered* where it went!" He popped it into his mouth and started to chew.

Was it bubblegum? Or raw hamburger?

Three dark-uniformed police officers came running into the restaurant. They raced into the kitchen with their hands on their holsters.

Staring at Monroe, I thought: *The monster you're looking for might be sitting right here with me.*

I shuddered.

I instantly felt bad for having that thought. I mean, Monroe was my new friend. That was no way to think about a friend.

Besides, I had no proof. I didn't know if the screaming woman was serious about seeing a monster. No one in the restaurant knew what to believe, either.

The kitchen doors were open wide. I saw a woman in a white apron and chef's hat. She was surrounded by people and the police listening to her talk. She waved her hands wildly in the air as she told her story.

The police officers left, shaking their heads. The restaurant grew calm again. That was it. No proof. What if I was wrong? I decided not to tell anyone — not even Lissa — till I had definite proof about Monroe.

Our cheeseburgers finally arrived. Monroe wolfed down both of his while I was just starting on mine. Then he gobbled up two orders of fries. He asked if he could have some of my fries. He said his stomach was still growling.

He finished my fries and burped so hard, it knocked over his Coke. He grinned. "How about dessert?"

"No way," I said. I checked the time on my phone. "I have to get back to my dad."

Monroe burped again. His burps were long and raw. They sounded more like vomiting than burping. "Can I come with you?"

"Yeah. Sure." I led the way through the mall to Dad's pet shop. The macaw wasn't in the front window. He'd been replaced by three fuzzy gray kittens. They were rolling around, having a wrestling match. A good crowd gathered to watch.

I opened the door for Monroe, and we stepped into the store. I waved to Dad. He was behind the front counter, handing a large green bag of dog kibble to a woman. She wrapped it in her arms and walked past Monroe and me, out of the store.

"This is my friend Monroe," I told Dad. Dad ducked out from behind the counter and came over to us, wiping his hands on the legs of his khakis.

Monroe had his back turned. He was staring intently at a large glass cage. I saw several gerbils scrabbling around through the layer of shredded newspaper at the bottom.

"Hi, Monroe," Dad said.

Monroe nodded. He kept his eyes on the little brown gerbils.

Dad lifted the glass lid and pulled out a gerbil. He let the gerbil climb over his hand. "Too many of you little guys," he muttered.

Monroe smiled at Dad. "Yeah. You sure have a bunch of them," he said.

"They're climbing all over each other." Dad shook his head. "I really should put them in a larger cage. They just multiply too fast."

"They're cute," Monroe said, eyeing the gerbil in Dad's hand.

Dad set the gerbil down gently on the shredded newspaper on the cage bottom. "One is cute," he said. "Thirty? Not cute." He lowered the lid over the cage.

A mynah bird whistled on its perch against the wall.

"Murray hates it when he doesn't get all the attention," Dad said. He walked over and petted the bird's beak with one finger. The mynah made a cooing sound. "Hey, did you two have lunch?" Dad asked.

"Yeah. We ate at The Burger Balloon," I said.

"Rafael will be here to take over," Dad said. "Then we can go home." He turned to Monroe. "Would you like a ride?"

Monroe tossed back his long hair. "Yeah. Sure. Thanks a lot."

Dad motioned to the rear of the store. "Bean, come to the supply room for a sec. Help me move some big seed bags." He disappeared into the back.

"Look around," I told Monroe. "I'll be right back."

"No problem," he said.

I turned and started to jog to the supply room. I was nearly there when I turned back — and uttered a hoarse cry.

A creature. A big, fur-covered creature . . . it stood in the aisle.

At first, I thought it was a gorilla. But it stood tall like a human, and I could see the long yellow fangs poking down from its black lips. And its bloodred eyes. And I realized . . .

I realized it was the monster. The same ugly monster I'd seen running to school.

I froze in shock. In total horror.

And I watched it lift the gerbil cage lid with a fat, furry paw. It pulled out two gerbils and raised them high.

It held them by their tails. I watched them swinging together upside down in its grasp.

And then, the creature lowered the two gerbils into its open mouth and noisily chewed them up.

11

I felt sick. My stomach heaved. I pressed my hand over my mouth to keep my lunch down.

I spun away from the monster and stumbled into the supply room. "Dad? Dad?" My voice burst out high and shrill.

He had a huge bag of birdseed slung over his shoulder. He was carrying it to a pile of seed bags against the wall.

"Dad — come quick!"

He squinted at me. "What's the problem? A customer?"

"N-no," I stammered. "It's . . . it's . . ."

He lowered the bag to the floor, then followed me, wiping his hands again.

"Dad. Look —" I pointed to the front of the store.

No one there.

No monster. No Monroe. The store was empty.

Dad crinkled up his face. "Bean, what's up? What are you showing me?"

47

My mouth hung open. My heart was doing flip-flops in my chest.

"A . . . monster," I choked out in a whisper.

Dad groaned. "Oh, Bean. *Not* another imaginary monster. Is that why you dragged me out here?"

"No, I —" I took a breath. "It wasn't imaginary. And it *ate* two gerbils."

He walked over to the glass cage and peered inside. "They look fine to me."

"Dad, do you know how many gerbils were in the cage? I mean, did you keep count?"

Dad scrunched up his face, thinking. "No. Actually, I didn't keep count. I don't know how many are in there. Maybe thirty, I guess."

"Dad, I saw it. I —"

"Where's your friend Monroe?" Dad asked. "Maybe he saw the monster, too."

"Over here." I heard Monroe shout.

I stepped to the next aisle and saw him in front of the mynah bird. "I didn't know they could talk," Monroe said. "Murray and I have been having a great conversation — haven't we, Murray?"

"*Loser*," the bird chirped. "*Loser*."

Dad laughed. "I taught him to say that. He knows a lot of words."

"Monroe, did you see anyone come into the store?" I demanded breathlessly.

He brushed his hair off his forehead. "No. No one."

48

"Are you sure?" My voice cracked. "Didn't you see something at the gerbil cage? Something standing over the cage?"

Monroe shook his head. "No. I had my back turned. I was talking to the bird the whole time you were gone."

"*Loser*," Murray chimed in. He obviously liked that word.

"Didn't you *hear* anything?" I cried.

Monroe shook his head again.

Dad put a hand on my shoulder. "Calm down, Bean."

"What's the problem?" Monroe asked.

"Bean has a monster problem," Dad told him. "He has monsters on the brain."

"Dad, that's not fair," I snapped. I studied Monroe. *Monroe is lying. He has to be lying.*

Murray the mynah bobbed his head up and down. "*Happy New Year!*" he declared.

Dad and Monroe burst out laughing. "Who taught him *that*?" Dad said. "Not me."

I didn't laugh. I could still see that gorilla-size monster sliding the two gerbils into his mouth. Why wouldn't Dad believe me? I wanted to scream. Aren't your parents supposed to *believe* you?

I really wanted Monroe to be my friend. But the monster seemed to appear wherever Monroe went. The school . . . the hamburger restaurant . . . the pet shop.

49

Was I really supposed to believe that Monroe wasn't a monster?

But that didn't make sense at all. He seemed like a totally normal guy. Why would a totally normal guy keep turning into a monster?

I kept thinking about this all the way home. My brain just kept turning it over and over. It was a mystery, a mystery I had to solve. I couldn't think about anything else.

I knew I had to try to take my mind off it. Dad dropped us off at home and left to do some errands.

"Can I hang out at your place?" Monroe asked. "No one is at my apartment."

I stared at him. I had to say yes. I couldn't let him know that I suspected him of being a monster. "Uh . . . sure," I said. "Come on up."

Mom was away, so the place was empty. I showed Monroe the new 3-D game-player my parents had given me for my birthday. We played some racing games for a while. Monroe beat me every time because my mind wasn't really into it.

My mind was still back at the pet store with the monster chewing up the gerbils, crunching their tiny bones in its teeth.

I wanted to ask Monroe about it again. I wanted to demand that he tell me the *truth*.

But I couldn't. Not because I was chicken. But because I didn't want him to think I was totally nuts.

Monroe left around five. I followed him into the hall. "Catch you later," I said. "Fun day."

"Yeah. Fun day." He didn't wait for the elevator. He went thudding down the stairs.

I stepped back into my apartment and closed the door carefully behind me. I let out a long sigh. I was so relieved that nothing bad had happened. Monroe had acted like a normal guy.

Later that night, I went into the kitchen and drank down a whole bottle of apple juice. I decided to call Lissa and tell her about what I saw in the pet store. I needed to ask her what I should do about Monroe.

I walked into my room and clicked on the light. Then I pulled out my phone and started to sit down on the edge of my bed.

"Whoa."

Something caught my eye. Something on my desk next to my laptop.

I crossed to the desk. Stopped. Held my breath. And stared.

Stared at a dead gerbil, its little body curled and stiff. And two words scrawled in red marker on the desk: *MONSTERS RULE*.

12

"Mom! Dad!" I screamed for my parents.

I heard their footsteps thudding in the hall. They burst into my room. "Bean? What is it?" Mom cried.

I couldn't speak. I jabbed a finger at the dead gerbil on my desk. "L-look," I managed to choke out.

They both stepped up to the desk, squinting at the dead animal and the scrawled words.

"I don't believe it!" Dad cried. "Do you . . . do you think that gerbil came from my shop?" He leaned down to eye it more closely.

"I — I don't know," I stammered.

"I'll get paper towels and wrap it up," Mom said softly.

Dad nodded.

"Who was in here?" I shouted. "Who came into my room? Who *did* this?"

Mom motioned with both hands for me to lower

my voice. "I'll get it cleaned up," she said. "No problem."

"But don't you care who *did* it?" I said.

"Guess someone really wanted to scare you," Dad said, rubbing his chin.

"Guess it worked!" I said. "Someone knows I have a monster problem. Someone —"

Mom disappeared to the kitchen. Dad stayed leaning over the desk, staring at the gerbil corpse.

My brain was whirring so hard I thought steam would shoot out of my ears. *Monroe. It had to be Monroe.*

"Monroe was here," I muttered. "This afternoon."

Dad squinted at me. "So?"

"Just saying," I replied.

He shrugged. "Monroe is your friend, right?"

"Yeah. But —"

I stopped. I didn't want to get into it with my parents about Monroe. I didn't have any proof. And if I told them I thought he was some kind of furry monster, they'd laugh at me. They'd tell me I was imagining things again.

Mom hurried back in and wrapped the dead gerbil in a paper towel. It was starting to smell really gross. I knew the smell would stay even after the body was gone.

Mom got a sponge and wiped away the two red words. She shook her head. "Bean, what do you think is going on here? Do you have any idea?"

"No. I don't know. I really don't. I just know this is going to give me bad dreams for a *week*!"

I wasn't lying. I had a horrible nightmare that night.

In this dream, I wasn't in the water. This time, I was running through our neighborhood. It was night, very dark, very cold. And I heard someone laughing. Hard, cruel laughter.

I ran to get away from it. But the laughter followed, close behind me. I covered both ears with my hands and ran as hard as I could.

But I couldn't escape it. The laughter grew louder until it became a roar. Monster laughter. And I knew the monster was right behind me.

I was afraid to turn around. I struggled to run faster. I ran behind houses, through hedges. I ripped through backyards and down a long alley, gravel crunching under my sneakers.

Go away. Please — stop laughing! Stop following me!

Again, I knew I was dreaming. As I ran, I struggled, I concentrated hard, trying to wake up, to pull myself out of the nightmare. But no.

The neighborhood disappeared and now I was thundering through dark woods. My shoes slid over a thick bed of dry leaves. Tree trunks, blacker than the night, appeared to bend toward me, as if trying to block my path.

And still, the terrifying laughter in my ears.

I gasped. Who was that standing against a fat tree? I ran right past him. I squinted, trying to focus. *Who is standing there? Who is in my dream?*

Harlan. Yes. Harlan. Standing with one hand on the tree trunk, watching me as I ran past him. His face a blank. And then he grinned when he saw how frightened I was. A big, toothy grin.

But Harlan didn't laugh. He only stared, happy at seeing my fear. He disappeared behind me as I ran farther into the woods. I ran until I couldn't run any more.

My chest felt about to burst. My legs wouldn't move another step. My head throbbed.

I had no choice. I spun around. I turned to face the monster. My whole body shuddered and shook.

Too dark to see clearly. The trees blocked out the sky and sent a heavy shadow over me, blacker than ink.

But I could see its red eyes. The monster's eyes glowed as if on fire. And I could see the outline of its broad, fur-covered body. And I could see it raise one giant paw — and point it at me.

It pointed at me, eyes blazing, and growled: *"You're next. You're NEXT!"*

13

I sat straight up in bed. My whole body shivered. I hugged myself, trying to stop shaking. I was drenched in sweat. It made my skin itch and tingle.

What did that MEAN?

Why did the monster say I was next?

It could mean only one thing — that I was its next victim.

"Only a dream," I murmured. But such a terrifying, real dream. So impossible to shake off.

And I knew it wasn't just a dream. I knew it meant something.

Pale morning sunlight washed in through my bedroom window. I raised my eyes to my desk. Somehow I expected the dead gerbil to be there again.

"Bean, you're late for school!" Mom's voice shook me out of my frightened thoughts.

"Huh? Late?"

"I've been on the phone. I forgot to wake you up. Hurry!"

"Mom — I had another nightmare. Can I tell you about it?"

No answer. She had gone back to the kitchen.

I pulled on the jeans and the T-shirt I'd tossed on the floor last night. I ran a brush through my hair a few times, then hurried to the kitchen for breakfast.

Dad was mopping a spot on his shirt with a wet napkin. He spills coffee on himself almost every morning.

Mom was on the phone, pacing back and forth as she talked. She pulled the phone away and said to Dad, "NASA wants me for two weeks. In Florida. I think I have to go."

"Maybe we *both* should go," Dad said. "Make it a vacation."

Mom put the phone back to her ear and continued talking.

"I have to tell you something about Monroe," I said. I didn't mean to say it. The words kind of tumbled from my mouth. But I couldn't hold my suspicions in any longer. I had to tell Mom and Dad my problem with Monroe.

Mom disappeared into the hall, talking on the phone the whole while. She always moved from room to room when she had an important call.

Dad frowned. "Guess I have to change this shirt. The spot isn't coming out."

"Can I tell you about Monroe?" I asked.

He glanced at the clock above the kitchen sink. "Oh, wow, Bean. You're really late. Here. Grab a protein bar and get going. If you run, you should get there in time."

"But, Dad —"

He shoved one of those horrible, sticky grain bars in my hand and gave me a push toward the door. "Okay, I'm going. I'm going." I grabbed my backpack and waved to Mom, still on the phone. "But I had a nightmare and I think Monroe —"

"Later," Dad called from the kitchen. "Have a good day, Bean."

I took the stairs to the first floor and stepped outside. It was a hot day already. The sun beat down, and the air felt heavy and wet.

I shifted my backpack on my back and started to walk. A squirrel stared up at me from the grass along the sidewalk. I broke off a piece of the protein bar and tossed it to him. He ran away. He didn't want to eat it, either.

I was halfway down the next block when I heard footsteps. I turned and saw Monroe jogging to catch up to me. "How's it going?" he called.

I shrugged. "I had a bad night."

"Bad night?" He brushed his hair off his forehead. He wore a black T-shirt with a yellow

58

frowny face on it and baggy black cargo pants. As always, he carried his lunch in a big brown paper bag.

I studied his face, trying to see if he knew about the dead gerbil on my desk. If he grinned or if his eyes flashed, I'd know he was the one who put it there.

But his face was a blank.

I had to ask. "Monroe, did you bring a gerbil home from my dad's store?"

"Excuse me?" His mouth dropped open. "A gerbil? Why? Is one missing?"

He seemed really surprised. Could I believe him?

"You didn't take a gerbil from the store?" I stared into his eyes.

"Well . . ." He hesitated. "Yes, I took one. And I have three more in my lunch bag."

14

"Huh?" I staggered back. "Are you *kidding* me?"

He grinned. "Of *course* I'm kidding you, lame-brain. Why would I steal a gerbil? What would I do with it?"

"Well . . ." I couldn't keep my eyes off his lunch bag.

Monroe laughed. "Are you totally losing it? You didn't *believe* me — did you?"

I didn't have a chance to answer. Harlan popped up in front of us from behind a clump of high shrubs. Like a wide tank, blocking our way. He wore a long-sleeved black shirt with the words BE AFRAID in bright red on the front.

He nodded to me, then turned his attention to Monroe. "Hey, dude. Your mom makes awesome lunches," he said. A grin spread over his fat face. "Have you got one of those awesome lunches for me today?"

Harlan made a grab for Monroe's lunch bag. But Monroe swiped it out of Harlan's reach.

Harlan growled like an angry animal. "You shouldn't have done that, dude."

Monroe's face turned bright red. He began gnashing his teeth. He hunched his whole body.

Like a dog getting ready to attack, I thought.

Or a monster.

Once again, I pictured the big, dark-furred creature in my dad's pet shop. I pictured him lifting the gerbils out of the case and sliding them into his gaping mouth.

Was it Monroe? It *had* to be Monroe.

Watching him seethe and boil, I knew what he was about to do. He was about to transform into a monster and *devour* Harlan.

I didn't like Harlan. In fact, I thought of him as my biggest enemy. But I didn't want to see him get *eaten*.

And what if I *did* see it? What if I did discover Monroe's secret for sure? Would Monroe have to eat me, too? Because I knew too much?

My frightening thoughts made me suddenly feel cold all over. The sky darkened. Heavy clouds rolled over the sun. I shivered.

"Think you're a tough guy?" Harlan sneered at Monroe.

He didn't give Monroe a chance to answer. He grabbed him by both shoulders — and *heaved* him off his feet.

Monroe uttered an angry cry as Harlan dragged him behind the tall shrubs.

Frozen in my place, I heard them scuffle. I heard low growls and grunts. I watched the leafy bush shake.

"Stop! Stop it!" I tried to scream, but my voice came out high and weak.

I knew what was happening. Harlan thought he was the toughest guy in school. But he was no match for a monster.

"Stop it!" I cried again. And finally, I was able to move.

I darted around the bush to see what was happening — and uttered a horrified gasp.

"Oh, no. Oh, noooo," I moaned.

Monroe stood there, hunched over. Panting like a dog.

And Harlan? There *was no* Harlan. No Harlan. No Harlan.

And then I lowered my eyes — and stared at a pile of bones on the ground.

15

I gagged. I grabbed my throat to keep from barfing.

Still panting, Monroe stood up straight. His face was red. He gave me a strange smile. It wasn't really a smile. It was like he didn't know what to do with his face.

I pointed to the pile of yellow bones. "H-Harlan?" I stammered.

And then I saw a flash of movement. I raised my eyes and saw Harlan running down the street. He was rocketing along the sidewalk, holding Monroe's lunch bag in front of him in one hand.

"Phheeeeew." I let out a long sigh of relief. I began to feel a little more normal.

I turned back to Monroe. He was breathing quietly again, and his face was no longer red. "What are these bones?" I demanded.

He gazed down at them and shrugged. "Beats me. Someone must have had chicken or something and dumped their garbage here. That's sick, isn't it?"

"Yeah. Sick," I said. I stared hard at him. He looked like a normal kid.

Monroe rubbed his shoulders. "Harlan really hurt me," he murmured. "What a jerk." He kicked the pile of bones under the bush.

"You just handed over your lunch to him?" I said.

He nodded. "Yeah. What choice did I have? That guy is a *monster*."

That word again. I shook my head. "We're both going to starve to death because of him."

"And he'll get bigger and bigger," Monroe said.

We started walking toward school. "Ever since he saved my life, he thinks he owns me," I said. "He says I'll be his slave for the rest of my life."

"He isn't kidding," Monroe said. "You and I will probably never eat lunch again."

"Maybe we should report him to Miss Hingle. You know. The principal."

Monroe suddenly stopped walking. He turned to me, and his expression turned to a scowl. "Don't worry about Harlan," he growled in a deep voice. "His time will come."

16

Lissa got a new video game called *Battle Tennis*, so I went up to her apartment to help her try it out. She's a good tennis player, and I'm good at war games. So it was a pretty close match.

Her apartment is bigger than mine. Her brother and sister each have a room of their own. But the two little kids didn't disappear to their rooms. They hung out with us in Lissa's room and pestered us until we turned the game controllers over to them.

They like a game called *Rock Guitar Dance Party*. It's the only game they play. And they always get into huge screaming fights over it.

We went into the kitchen and grabbed two Cokes and a bag of tortilla chips. Then we sat across from each other on tall stools at the kitchen counter. I could hear the two kids already arguing over the game down the hall.

"Little monsters." Lissa chuckled.

"Speaking of monsters . . ." I started.

She rolled her eyes. "*Now* what? Are you going to tell me you're seeing monsters again?"

"Listen to me," I said. "And stop crunching the chips so loud. I can't hear myself talk."

"Grouchy much?" she said. "Are you coming to my swim meet on Friday?"

"Don't change the subject," I said.

"I want you to come watch me swim Friday. You're such a loser, Bean. You could have been on the boys' team. You could have had a good time. It's way more fun than sneaking around looking for monsters."

I jumped off the kitchen stool. "Did you just call me a loser?"

Her cheeks turned pink. "I meant it in a nice way."

"Lissa, someone put a dead gerbil in my room."

She stopped chewing. She stared at me. She took a long sip from her soda can, eyeing me the whole time.

"Bean, a dead gerbil? In your room?"

"On my desk. Dead. Totally stiff," I said. "Someone put it there. Do you believe it? Someone killed a gerbil and put it in my room."

She blinked. "Are you sure it didn't die of natural causes?"

She tossed her head back and burst out laughing.

"How funny are you?" I said. "Not."

"Maybe it wandered in from the street and had a heart attack when it saw your room." She laughed some more.

"Great friend," I muttered. "Big joke. Ha-ha."

She forced herself to stop laughing. "Sorry. Really."

"Whoever did it scrawled two words on my desk. *Monsters Rule*."

She took another long drink from the soda can. "So someone was messing with you. Someone who knows you're afraid of monsters. Any idea who?"

"Monroe," I said.

She rolled her eyes again. "Always Monroe. Bean, I thought you wanted him to be your new best friend."

"I do want him to be my best friend. But not if he keeps turning into a hairy monster."

She chuckled. "What if he's a *friendly* monster?"

"Lissa, stop making jokes," I snapped. "It isn't funny. You wouldn't like it if someone came into your room and left a dead animal there."

She patted my shoulder. "Sorry." She stared at me while she chewed some more tortilla chips. "I have an idea, Bean."

I frowned at her. "What kind of idea?"

"Why don't you just go up to Monroe and ask him if he's a monster?"

67

"Aaaaaagggh." I let out a cry. "Great idea," I said. "Great way to lose a friend forever. What if I ask him the question and he *isn't* a monster? He'll think I'm crazy."

"Everyone already thinks you're crazy," Lissa said.

"Oh, wow. You're going to bring up the swimming pool thing again?"

"Just saying."

"What am I going to do?" I cried. I slammed my Coke can on the counter. "Last night, the monster in my dream pointed at me and growled, '*You're next. You're next.*' What does that mean? Does some monster want to *kill* me? I . . . I think I'm really in danger, Lissa."

Her expression turned serious. "Wish I could help you," she said softly. Then her eyes grew wide.

I realized she wasn't looking at me. She was staring over my shoulder.

Before I could turn around, she opened her mouth in a scream of horror.

17

I spun around. I stared at the kitchen doorway. No one there.

Lissa dropped off the kitchen stool. She pointed. "I . . . I saw it. It was there."

I stared at the empty doorway. "What? You saw what?"

"Quick, Bean." She grabbed my hand and pulled me into the hall. We looked both ways. No one there. I could hear the little kids dancing to their dance party game.

"Lissa, I don't see anything."

She trotted to the front door and checked the lock. "I saw it. The monster. It . . . it was here, Bean. It followed you."

I swallowed hard. I suddenly felt cold all over. "You saw it? Really?"

She nodded. Her whole body shuddered. "It was big and hairy. I mean, covered in dark fur. Like a gorilla or something. Only, its eyes were human. Red eyes. It looked ugly . . . ugly and mean."

A thousand questions spun through my mind. "But how did it get in, Lissa? Where did it go?"

She shrugged. "It appeared and then it disappeared. But I saw it. I believe you now. And I believe it followed you here."

"You mean . . . you finally think it's real?"

She nodded. She squeezed my arm. "You didn't make it up. It was real." She pressed her back against the wall. I could see she was thinking hard. "Maybe it *is* Monroe. Monroe lives in this building. He knows I live here, too. Maybe he followed you."

"Wh-what am I going to do?" I stammered.

"Follow him," she answered.

"Huh? What do you mean?"

"Follow Monroe. Spy on him. Watch him when he thinks no one is watching. Because . . ."

"Because I have to prove he's the monster?"

"Yes. You have to prove it. You have to see if you're right about him."

I nodded, thinking hard. "There's only one problem with that," I told her.

"Problem?"

"Yeah. What if I *am* right? What then?"

18

"Have you ever been to Lissa's apartment?" I asked Monroe.

It was the next morning, and we were walking to school.

Harlan had already bombed up to us. He said he was going to give us both a break today. So he took *both* of our lunches. We watched helplessly as he ran off laughing like a maniac.

Sweet guy.

I'd been thinking about my plan to spy on Monroe and learn the truth about him. As we walked along Elm Street, I felt kind of jumpy. Excited. But not a good kind of excited. Just tense.

Monroe scratched his cheek. "No. Never been to her apartment. It's on six, right?"

How did he know the floor Lissa lived on?

I nodded. "Yeah. It's nice. It has a long hall with lots of rooms. Bigger than my apartment." I squinted at him, trying to read his thoughts. "You never been there?"

71

"No. Lissa seems nice. But she never talks to me."

We let a school bus rumble past. Then we crossed the street.

I remembered the first time I saw the monster. Running toward the school entrance. It was in a flash of bright sunlight. Yes. The sun was so bright, I had to blink. And when I could focus again, I saw the monster.

"Let's cross the street," I said. I tugged him by the arm.

He pulled back. "Why? We never walk on that side."

"It's sunnier," I said. "I just feel like a little sun." *If we walk in the bright sunlight, maybe you'll turn furry again.*

I pulled him across the street. The morning sun was still low in the sky, and it was blindingly bright.

I blinked a few times. Just the way I had the first time. I shut my eyes for a few seconds. And when I opened them . . .

. . . When I opened them, Monroe looked exactly the same. No fur. No monster.

I felt disappointed. And relieved. All at the same time. It made my stomach feel funny, like all churned up.

I don't like spying on my friends. But what choice did I have?

You're next. You're next.

I couldn't get that growled threat out of my ears. I heard it over and over. And each time, it gave me a chill.

In class, it was easy to keep an eye on Monroe. Because he sat at the desk right next to me.

We had quiet reading hour just before lunch. I was reading a book called *The Call of the Wild*. I like animal stories, and this was a great one about a dog.

Suddenly, I gasped when I heard Monroe let out a growl.

My book fell onto the desk. I turned, expecting him to be furry.

He grinned at me and rubbed his stomach. "Can you hear my stomach growling?" he whispered. "I'm so hungry."

"Mine is growling, too," I lied.

His stomach growled again. "Too bad Harlan stole our lunches," he muttered. He went back to his book. I glanced at the cover. He was reading *Frankenstein*.

Later, I borrowed some money from Lissa and bought lunch for me and Monroe. I watched him eat his ham sandwich and bag of potato chips. He didn't do anything unusual.

Some kids at the next table were having a burping contest. It made Monroe smile, but he didn't join in. I never took my eyes off him. I looked for any sign. But he didn't do anything the tiniest bit monsterish.

Lissa stepped up beside me in the hall after lunch. "How's it going?" she whispered.

"Nothing yet," I said.

"Keep watching him, Bean. Don't give up. You have to know the truth, right?"

"Right."

She grabbed my arm. "But be careful. Don't let him know you're spying on him."

"No way," I said.

What would he do if he knew?

I tried to be careful. Whenever Monroe glanced my way, I pretended to be watching something else. I was totally tense, but I tried to seem perfectly calm and normal.

"Are you enjoying the *Frankenstein* book?" I asked him.

"It's kind of hard to read," he said. "But I like monster stories."

Really?

Not much of a clue. I mean, lots of people like monster stories. Including me.

The day dragged by without anything interesting happening. Until gym class late that afternoon.

Coach Waller had a bunch of us guys playing a basketball game at one end of the gym. It was shirts and skins, and I was happy to be on the skins team because it was steamy and hot in the gym.

Monroe played on the other team. He was a

74

very aggressive player. He kept bumping and shouldering and even head-butting other players. I could see Waller watching him from the sidelines. Monroe was playing harder than anyone else.

He was a total ball hog. He kept driving to the basket, and never passed the ball to another teammate. He took shot after shot — and sank most of them.

I was surprised. I'd never thought of him as being a sports dude.

Sweat matted his thick hair and poured down his forehead. His face was bright red, and he kept making grunting sounds as he ran up and down the court.

Is this a clue? Is he finally going to reveal himself?

"Whoa!" I missed a pass. It bounced off my chest because I had my eye on Monroe.

"Bean — are you a klutz or a super klutz?" a kid named Arnie shouted.

"Both," I said. It was supposed to be a joke, but no one laughed.

I shoved my arms out to block Monroe, but he dribbled right past me as if I were invisible. Kids cheered as he dropped another basket.

Then, to my surprise, he walked right off the basketball floor. His chest was heaving up and down because he was breathing really hard. He had his eyes on the locker room door.

This is it, I told myself. *I'm about to get my proof.*

Yes, it was just a hunch. But it was a strong hunch. As I saw Monroe slump into the locker room, I knew he was about to turn into a monster and do something weird.

I tossed the ball to Arnie, gave the players a little wave, and trotted to the locker room. "Back in a minute," I called to Coach Waller.

I grabbed the door handle and pulled the locker room door open just a crack. I didn't want Monroe to know I was following him.

I peered inside. The air was cooler in there. The locker room was nearly dark. I could hear showers running in the back. I stepped inside and closed the door silently behind me. I didn't see Monroe in the row of gym lockers.

The back of my neck began to tingle. A drop of sweat fell from my nose. I realized I was holding my breath. I stepped on tiptoe toward the back of the dressing room.

I stopped when I heard the shuffle of sneakers in the next row of lockers. I waited . . . waited . . .

And then I heard a scream. A high, shrill shriek of pain.

And I knew . . . I knew. *The monster has attacked someone.*

19

I took a deep breath and took off. I ran to the next aisle and stared down the row of lockers.

I knew I was about to see something ugly. Something horrifying.

But . . . no. It was a kid in my class. A short, skinny, red-haired guy named Victor. He stood hunched in front of an open locker, shaking his right hand. He turned when he saw me. "Bean?"

"I . . . heard a scream," I stammered.

He nodded. He raised his hand. "I just slammed it in the locker. That was me screaming. It hurts. Man, it really hurts."

I struggled to catch my breath. I stared at Victor's hand. It was swelling up like a balloon. "You'd better show it to Coach Waller," I said.

He nodded. He started toward the door.

"Have you seen Monroe?" I called after him.

He motioned with his head to the back.

I spotted Monroe at a sink in front of the shower room. He was splashing cold water on his face. He turned when I stepped close.

"My face started to burn," he said, water running down the front of his shirt. "Guess I got overheated." He squinted at me. "What are *you* doing here? Why'd you leave the game?"

"I . . . uh . . . was worried about you," I said. "I saw you leave and I thought maybe you were sick."

"Hey, thanks." He splashed more water over his hair. "Thanks a lot, Bean. You're a good friend."

We walked back to the gym floor together. Monroe had this strange smile on his face. Like he was pleased with himself about something.

And as we joined the game, I found myself thinking:

Did I make a terrible mistake about Monroe?

Or is he behaving himself because he figured out I'm watching him?

Those are the questions I wanted to ask Lissa when I met up with her outside the school swimming pool before her team practice.

She kept swinging her swim bag, hitting me in the knees with it.

"Do you have to do that?" I asked.

She grinned. "Yes, I do." She swung it again, and I dodged out of the way.

"Are you coming to my swim meet tomorrow?" she asked.

"Is there a meet tomorrow?" I said. "You've only told me about it twenty times."

She hit me with the blue canvas bag again. "Are your underpants too tight? Is that why you're in such a bad mood?"

"I don't want to talk about my underpants with a girl," I said. "I'm in a bad mood because I've been spying on Monroe all day, and it's a total waste of time. I think maybe he guessed I'm spying on him."

"Maybe," she said. "But do you always have to be a quitter, Bean? You've only been spying one day. You've got to keep it up."

I jumped away from her swim bag as it came around again. "Okay. So now I'm a loser and a quitter?"

"I don't want to talk about it," Lissa said. "You're going to make me late. Listen, have you thought about the school pet fair?"

"Yeah. A little," I said.

Two girls from the swim team trotted past, hurrying to the pool. They both laughed when they saw me. I knew why. They were remembering me standing at the pool with my swimsuit down at my ankles.

I could feel myself blushing all over again.

"Well, for sure *I'm* not going to win the three-hundred-dollar prize," Lissa said. "All I've got is my boring cat, Corky. But you've got a whole pet shop to choose from."

"Yeah, I know," I said. "I wanted to bring a mynah bird. But my dad has an aquarium with some betta fighting fish. He said they can't lose. They are totally fierce and awesome to watch."

"Cool," Lissa said. "You'll probably win." She spun away and, still swinging the swim bag, headed to the pool. "Maybe winning the pet fair will put you in a better mood," she called without looking back.

"Maybe," I said.

Did I know then that the day of the pet fair was going to be the *worst day* of my life?

No. I didn't have a clue.

20

I climbed the stairs to our apartment. I almost never take the elevator. It's too slow. It creaks and groans as if it's complaining about having to carry people.

Since I live on the fourth floor, it isn't very far to go. Monroe doesn't have to climb at all since he lives on the first floor of the building.

I wondered if he was home. I wondered if he was in his room, changing into a growling monster. I wondered if he liked to roar and thrash the air with his big paws and terrify his little brother and sister.

But what if *they* were monsters, too?

What if the whole Morton family were monsters?

"What if I'm going crazy?" I said to myself as I opened our apartment door.

"Talking to yourself?" Mom said, turning as I entered. "That's the first sign."

I jumped. I didn't expect her to be home. She's usually at her office, thinking about rockets all day.

"Oh, h-hi," I stammered. "I didn't think —"

She was arranging yellow and white flowers in a vase. "Aren't these pretty? I saw them at the market, and I had to buy them. They smell nice, too."

I dropped my backpack on the floor. I sniffed the air. Yes, they smelled sweet.

"How was your day?" Mom asked, working at the flowers.

"Not bad," I said. And then I blurted out what was on my mind. "You know, I had another monster nightmare. And in the dream, the monster pointed at me and said, '*You're next. You're next.*' I know it sounds crazy, but I think Monroe is a monster. And I think he's dangerous. I think maybe he's very dangerous. So I've been spying on him. You know. Trying to prove for sure that he's a monster."

It felt so good to finally get the words out. It just felt great to get the whole thing off my chest.

Mom turned to me. She shook her head. "I'm sorry, Bean. This song is so loud in my ears, I didn't hear a word you just said."

She pulled the little white earphones from her ears. "Now, tell me again. What were you saying?"

"Well —"

The phone rang.

Mom started toward the kitchen. "I'd better get that. I've been expecting a call from Houston."

I let out a long whoosh of air. I suddenly felt like a deflated balloon. I could hear Mom talking on the phone. She just kept saying *yes, yes, yes.* Who knows what that was about.

When you're a rocket scientist, you get a lot of calls from Florida and from Houston and Washington. People are always calling and asking her advice.

Dad gets calls, too. It's usually about sick pets. Or pets that died. Dad says he just sells pets, he doesn't doctor them. But people call anyway.

I dragged my backpack into my room. I checked the desk to make sure there were no dead animals there. That's what I thought about every time I walked into my room. *Will I find another dead gerbil?*

My next thought: *Is the monster coming for me? Am I really NEXT?*

I shivered. I wasn't safe — not even in my own bedroom.

I walked to my bedroom window and pushed aside the curtains. The window looked down on the street.

Whoa. I could see Harlan down there. He was talking to two blond-haired girls. I couldn't see their faces. Just the tops of their heads.

Harlan shoved one of them really hard, and she toppled onto the sidewalk. Her friend pulled her to her feet, and they both ran away.

Harlan acts like a monster all the time. I suddenly remembered what Lissa said to me. She said if I ever stood up to Harlan, my nightmares about being chased by a monster would stop.

That's because I told her I thought Harlan was the monster in my dreams. But that was before Monroe moved in.

"Bean — can you do me a favor?" Mom shouted from the kitchen.

I turned away from the window and made my way down the hall. "What's the favor?"

"Run down to the store on the corner and buy sour cream. You know your dad likes sour cream on his baked potato. And I completely forgot to buy it."

"No problem," I said.

She handed me a twenty-dollar bill. "Just get a small container. You and he are the only ones who eat it."

I nodded and headed out the door. I tucked the money in my jeans pocket and started down the stairs. I could hear voices in the stairwell from one of the floors below.

I went past the second floor landing, turned, and started down to the first floor. But I stopped halfway when I heard strange sounds.

Not talking.

I heard a grunt. Then a low growl.

I gripped the banister. It sounded like two dogs were having a fight down there.

I peered down. The curve of the stairway hid them from sight.

I heard an angry snarl. And then the sound of teeth gnashing. A squeal. Another squeal. Hard thumps. Like someone bumping the wall. And then two throaty growls.

I held my breath and listened.

Could there be a dogfight in the stairwell?

My legs trembled. I gripped the banister tighter.

I had to see what was going on down there.

Loud growls erupted. More thumps and bumps.

I lowered myself to the next stair. Then one more. Slowly, carefully, I crept down the stairway, gripping the banister tightly in my cold, clammy hand.

The stairs turned. I stopped and stared. Stared in horror at *three* ugly monsters.

Red-eyed. Covered in dark fur like gorillas. Growling and wrestling on the concrete floor. Swiping at each other. Snapping their long teeth playfully.

Yes. They were playing. Three ugly, growling monsters wrestling for fun.

"Noooo." A frightened moan escaped my throat. I spun around and started to run up the stairs.

Did they hear me?

I heard growls and thuds.

Yes. They were coming after me.

My foot missed a step. I fell forward. Fell hard. Banged my knees on the metal stair. My glasses flew off.

They had me. No way to escape them.

I shut my eyes and waited for them to pounce.

21

After a few terrifying seconds, I raised my head. I looked behind me.

No monsters.

I could hear their noisy wrestling match below. Their growls echoed up the narrow stairwell.

They hadn't seen me.

Quickly, I pulled myself up. My knees throbbed. I rubbed them. I could feel blood on my leg. I'd cut both knees.

Ignoring the pain, I grabbed my glasses and pulled myself back up the three flights to my apartment. I let myself in, breathing hard.

"Mom — monsters!" My voice came out choked and small.

She came into the hallway, wiping her hands on a red-and-white dish towel. "Bean? Back so soon? Where's the sour cream?"

"M-monsters," I stuttered. I pointed frantically. "At the bottom of the stairs. Three of them."

Mom's expression turned angry. "Bean, I don't have time for this now. Dinner is going to be late."

"No. Mom. Please —" I pleaded. "Please listen to me. They're down there. I saw them. They —"

She folded the towel between her hands. "Deal with them, Bean."

I gasped. "Huh? Deal with them? Mom, what does that mean?"

She didn't answer. I grabbed her arm. My hand was icy and damp. "Come with me. Hurry. I'll show you."

She pulled back. "Bean, I'm not happy about this. I'm trying to prepare dinner."

"Just come with me!" I screamed. I tugged her hard toward the apartment door.

"Okay, okay. I'm coming."

I led the way onto the landing. "Three monsters," I said. "You'll see. You'll see I'm not making it up." I started down the first flight of stairs.

She followed close behind. "Are you sure —?"

I raised a finger to my lips. "Sssshhh. They'll hear us."

"But, Bean —"

"Mom. Sshhh. They'll hear us. They'll attack," I whispered.

My heart was racing. I didn't want to go back down there. But I had to prove to Mom that I wasn't crazy. I had to show her what I'd seen. I had to make her *believe*.

I grabbed her hand as we drew close to the first floor. We followed the stairway as it curved.

"You'll see," I whispered. "You'll see."

We tiptoed silently down a few more stairs.

Mom squeezed my hand. Another step. Another.

And then I opened my mouth in a horrified cry.

22

The landing was empty. No monsters. No one.

Mom let go of my hand. She let out a sigh. "Bean, Bean, Bean," she whispered. "What am I going to do with you?"

"You — you've got to believe me," I stammered. "They were here. I saw them."

"Of course they were," she said. "There are monsters everywhere. Everywhere you look."

I scowled at her angrily. Why was she making fun of me? Why couldn't I get her to take the whole thing seriously? There were real monsters here. My life was in danger. And all she did was laugh at me.

I felt defeated. Weak and defeated. Too weak to argue with her.

She gave me a gentle push with both hands. "Go get the sour cream."

I tried to call Lissa that night, but she didn't answer her phone. I tried to think about other things. I didn't want to go crazy being obsessed with monsters day and night. But I couldn't concentrate on my math notebook. And I read a few chapters of *The Call of the Wild* without even seeing what I was reading.

Face it. I was totally messed up.

I kept thinking about Monroe and going over everything I'd seen. Every clue led to Monroe being a monster.

This afternoon, those three monsters were wrestling on the first floor. And where does Monroe's family live? On the first floor. They were wrestling just a few feet from his apartment.

Were they Monroe and his brother and sister?

What a mystery. My head was spinning. I was afraid to go to sleep. What if I had the monster dream again? What if the monster returned to my room, came to make me his next victim as he had promised?

I stayed up really late, and then I slept a deep sleep without any dreams.

The next day slid by in a blur. I struggled to listen to Mrs. Fielding and to do my schoolwork. But it was like my brain was in a different place.

Lissa's swim meet was after school. Monroe joined me as I crossed to the pool building. I didn't really want to be with him. Face it, I was totally scared of him now.

But I had no choice. I couldn't tell him I didn't want to sit with him.

I opened the doors and was greeted by a roar of voices. A big crowd of kids and teachers had come to watch the first girls' swim meet of the year.

Lissa was doing her warm-up in the deep end of the pool. She moved gracefully through the sparkling blue water. The ceiling lights reflected in the pool, like spotlights shimmering on the surface. She raised her head and waved to us. Then went back to her steady strokes.

I counted a dozen girls on our team. They all wore red-and-blue swimsuits, the school colors. When the other girls' team arrived from Harding Middle School, the pool became jammed with swimmers.

The voices, the whistles blowing, the laughter, the splashing water — the sounds rang loudly off the blue tile walls.

Monroe and I sat in the third row on the far end of the bleachers. He mopped his forehead with one hand. "It's hot in here," he said. "And the air is so wet." He wiped his sweat on my jeans leg.

"Hey, give me a break," I groaned. "Don't you love the smell of chlorine?"

"We should jump in the water," he said. "Cool off."

I squinted at him. "In our clothes?"

"It would be bold." He snickered.

"You go first," I said.

"Dare me?"

Was he *serious*?

We both laughed.

I was pretending everything was normal. I didn't want to give Monroe any clues that I was suspicious of him.

Miss Greene, the girls' team coach, blew her whistle, calling all the girls to the side. The Harding girls continued their warm-ups.

"Lissa is in the first event," I told Monroe. "She says it's her best chance. She really wants to win this race."

"Look at that girl!" Monroe said, pointing. He pointed to a Harding girl climbing out of the pool. She was big and powerful looking, and at least six feet tall. "Is she really in middle school? She's a *giant*!"

"Hope she isn't racing against Lissa," I said.

A few minutes later, I knew that it wasn't Lissa's day.

The tall, powerful Harding swimmer lined up to swim against her. Lissa was doomed.

She swam well. She did her best. But she was no match for the Harding girl. Lissa finished nearly half a lap behind her.

I watched Lissa slump unhappily at the side of the pool. Water dripped down her face. She didn't even bother wiping it from her eyes. She kept shaking her head and muttering to herself.

I felt bad. I knew the race meant a lot to her.

93

I wanted to go tell her what a good job she did. But the next race was starting. Lissa pulled herself from the pool and, still shaking her head, walked to the team bench.

"Too bad," Monroe said. "Lissa didn't stand a chance. That Harding girl could eat Lissa for lunch!"

Why did Monroe think so much about lunch? And eating humans? Was that a clue?

"Hey, I've got to go," he said. He jumped off the side of the bleacher. "I only came to see Lissa. Are you staying?"

I watched the next two girls start to swim. "Yeah, I'll stay," I said. "I want to wait and talk to Lissa."

"Later, dude." He disappeared behind the bleachers.

A cheer went up as the girl on our team reached the far end of the pool, kicked off the wall, and began to return. I turned and saw Lissa on the bench. Her head was down. She wasn't even watching.

A few of the races were close. But we lost almost all of them. The Harding team was just too strong.

After the last race, the teams strode into the locker rooms. The bleachers emptied. I climbed to my feet and began to pace back and forth along the side of the pool. I knew Lissa would come out, and I wanted to see her.

94

My footsteps echoed in the empty pool building. The only sound. The sudden silence felt strange. I kept my eyes on the locker room door as I walked back and forth along the pool edge.

"Huh?" I uttered a startled cry when I heard a heavy *splash*.

I turned toward the sound — and froze. A dark form rolled through the water, sending up low waves as it moved.

"Hey!" I shouted.

I stood at the deep end. The dark blob swam rapidly toward me. Like a seal. Or a walrus.

And then it raised itself in the water.

My knees went weak as I stared at the furry, clawed, red-eyed monster in front of me.

"Nooooo!" A scream escaped my throat.

I tried to stagger back. But my legs refused to work.

The creature was surprisingly fast.

It raised itself high. Leaped up from the water. Wrapped its big, furry arms around my waist. And pulled me into the pool.

23

The shock of the cold water made me freeze for a second.

The monster kept me close to its body and sank below the surface.

I held my breath as the water rose over my head. My heart pounded so hard, I could feel the blood pulsing in my ears.

I waited . . . waited for it to let go of me. But it held me tight, pressing me hard against the thick fur of its chest.

Did it plan to *drown* me?

I began to thrash my arms and legs. I tried to kick it . . . kick its legs. I squirmed and turned my head. I wanted to butt my head against it. Or *bite* it.

Wild colors swirled past me. Was I passing out? I knew I couldn't hold my breath much longer.

I raised both fists and pushed against its chest.

It held on tight. Bubbles escaped my mouth. My chest felt about to explode.

Frantic, I raised both hands — and raked my fingernails down the creature's front.

I felt it pull back. Its hold on me loosened.

I scraped my nails down its fur again, trying to dig deep into its flesh.

And *yes*. YES!

Its arms dropped away. It seemed to retreat.

I didn't give it a chance to recover. I slid free. Raised my hands and, kicking hard, forced my body to rise to the surface. Gasping, choking, I sucked in breath after breath.

I could see the inky, dark figure below me at the bottom of the pool. It was real. I wasn't imagining it.

I had to get out of there. But it was too fast for me. As I struggled to swim to the side of the pool, it bobbed to the surface. I turned and saw its red-eyed stare.

Water rolled down my face. I was still panting hard. But I stared back at it. And a hoarse scream burst from my throat.

"What do you *want*? Why are you here? Is that you, Monroe? Monroe? What do you *want*?"

The monster uttered a deep moan. *"Monroe?"* it snarled. Its voice was a dry rasp, like it was vomiting the word. *"Monroe?"*

"Yes. Are you Monroe?" I cried.

It stared hard at me. *"Maybe . . ."* it growled.

Then it dove at me. Wrapped its claws around my chest. Slashed through my clothes. Pulled me . . . pulled me down again.

It's going to drown me.

But no. It heaved me to the surface. I rose up, spluttering and choking.

I heard footsteps at the far end of the pool.

The monster heard them, too. It pointed at me and rasped: *"You're next. You're next!"*

My nightmare come true.

"You're NEXT!"

And then it shot past me, kicking hard, its red eyes still locked on me. It grabbed the side of the pool and hoisted itself up. The big body sent a tidal wave of water over me.

And when the wave had passed, the monster had vanished. I heard its clomping, heavy footsteps behind the bleachers.

"Wheeeeew." I let out a long whoosh of air. I turned toward the footsteps and saw Coach Greene come walking out of the locker room. She stopped when she saw me bobbing in the deep end of the pool.

"Bean?" Coach Greene shouted. "Bean? Is that you? What on earth! What are you doing in the pool?"

Think fast, Noah. Think fast.

"The breast stroke?" I said.

24

When I climbed out of the pool, I couldn't stop shaking. Part of it was the cold. Part of it was my fright at almost being drowned by a hideous monster.

Coach Greene found a blanket somewhere and wrapped it around me. She made me call home. Dad was there. He said he'd come pick me up in the car.

Lissa came out of the locker room and waited for my dad with me in front of the school. Coach Greene had told her what happened. Lissa kept her eyes on me, expecting me to explain. But I really didn't feel like talking.

"It . . . it was the monster," I said finally. "The one from my nightmares. It grabbed me and pulled me into the pool. It held me down. It tried to drown me."

"Wow," she murmured, shaking her head. "Wow. Are you going to tell your parents?"

"Yes," I said. I didn't have to think about it. I

mean, this time I nearly drowned. "I have to make them believe me. I need help. I'm not crazy. The monster said I'm next. It really wants to get me."

She was silent for a moment. I saw Dad's blue Ford Focus on the next block. He honked his horn. "Bean, do you still think it's Monroe?"

"Yes," I said. "It *has* to be Monroe. He left the swim meet early. Right after your race. He didn't really have a reason. He just disappeared."

"But *why* would Monroe do that? Why would he want to scare you? Why would he try to drown you?"

"Because he's a monster? Maybe he can't control himself. Maybe when the monster brain takes over, he has to kill and destroy. He has to act like a total beast."

Lissa bit her bottom lip. "Maybe," she murmured. "But I still don't think you have enough proof. I don't think you can say for sure that it's Monroe."

I couldn't talk about it any longer. Dad pulled the car to the curb in front of us. He pushed open the front door and stared at me with the blanket wrapped around me.

"Bean, what happened?" he asked.

"I'll tell you later," I said.

I decided to tell Mom and Dad at dinner.

I practiced in my room. I planned to keep my voice low and steady. I was going to start at the beginning. Tell them about Monroe running toward the school in sunlight, and how I suddenly saw a monster the size of a gorilla running where Monroe had run.

Then I'd calmly, quietly tell them about the monster in the hamburger restaurant at the mall. And then the monster eating the gerbils in Dad's store. I'd explain how that *had* to be Monroe. It *all* had to be Monroe.

This time, I'd make them believe me. This time, I'd convince them to help me.

"My nightmares are coming true," I planned to tell them. "There's a monster after me, and he won't stop until I'm as dead as that gerbil."

I rehearsed in my room, pacing back and forth. I stood at the window and peered down at the street. And planned what I was going to say.

Finally, Dad called from the kitchen. "Dinner, Bean. Your favorite tonight. Lamb chops."

I love lamb chops. I like picking them up in my hand and eating the meat off the bones. But tonight I didn't feel hungry at all.

"Mmmm. Smells good," I said. I took my place at the table.

Mom forked two lamb chops and a baked potato onto my plate. "So what happened at school this afternoon?" she asked. "Did you fall into the pool?"

"Tell us what's up with you," Dad said.

"Well . . ." I took a deep breath. "It's kind of a long story," I said.

"We have time for a long story," Dad said. He spooned some brussels sprouts onto his plate. "Go ahead."

"Well . . ." My throat suddenly felt dry. "I have to tell you something . . . about Monroe," I said.

"That's a coincidence," Mom said. "Because we have something to tell *you* about Monroe.

I dropped my fork. "Huh?"

"Mom has to go to Florida to do some work for NASA," Dad said. "She and I decided we'd make a vacation of it. We'll be gone for about a week. And guess what?"

"What?" I said.

"Monroe's family said you could go downstairs and live with them for the week," Mom said.

"L-live with Monroe?" I stammered.

"Yes," Mom said. "You and Monroe together for a whole week. Isn't that great?"

25

I felt sick. I could feel my heart sinking into my stomach. My head spun.

I gripped the edge of the table. "Please —" I choked out.

"Bean, you don't look happy," Mom said.

"It's just because he's surprised," Dad told her.

"No," I said. "You don't understand."

"We'll only be gone a week," Mom said. "You won't miss us that much."

"*You don't understand,*" I said through clenched teeth. "Monroe is a monster."

Mom and Dad laughed.

Dad picked up his fork and knife and began to cut his lamb chop. "We're so glad you've made a new friend," he said.

"Maybe Monroe will help you get over your fear of monsters," Mom said.

"No, he won't help me," I replied. "He won't help me because *he's* a monster."

"Stop being silly," Mom said. She shook her head. "Really, Bean. This has got to stop. You're seeing monsters everywhere you look."

"I have proof," I said.

That wasn't exactly true. I'd been trying to get proof. I didn't really have it yet. But I knew my hunch about Monroe had to be right.

He was a monster. A few hours before, he'd tried to drown me. And now they were sending me downstairs to live with him. Sending me into a total trap.

"I — I won't do it!" I cried. I didn't mean to sound so whiny. It just came out that way.

"That's enough," Dad snapped. He set down his silverware and narrowed his eyes at me. "Enough monster talk. Do you hear me?"

"Let's change the subject," Mom said, giving me a fake smile.

"I got in some new fighting fish at the store," Dad said. "They'll be perfect for your pet fair at school. You should win the prize easily."

"I'd rather be eaten by fighting fish than by a monster," I said.

"That's *enough*!" Dad shouted. He never shouts. I could see I was making him angry.

"Okay, okay," I muttered.

They weren't going to listen to me. Why start a big fight? Just because I probably wouldn't be alive when they got back home?

After dinner, they gave me a big travel bag and told me to go to my room and pack. I carried it into my room, flung it onto the bed, and closed my bedroom door.

Then I called Lissa. "You won't believe what's happening," I told her. "They're sending me downstairs to live with the monster for a week."

"Maybe it won't be so bad," she said.

"Huh? You, *too*?" I cried. "Why won't it be bad? Tell me. Didn't he try to drown me in the pool? Didn't he point at me and growl, '*You're next. You're next*'?"

"But you don't really know if the monster was Monroe," she argued. "It's just a hunch."

"It's not a hunch," I told her. "I asked him. I asked the monster. I said, '*Are you Monroe?*' And he looked at me and said '*Maybe*.' Like he was playing it cute."

"Doesn't Monroe have brothers and sisters?" Lissa asked.

"Yes," I said.

"Well, he won't act like a monster with them around."

"Sure, he will," I said. "I think *they're* monsters, too. I think I saw them in the stairwell, and —"

Lissa laughed.

"Lissa," I said, "I don't understand why you're not taking this seriously. Don't you understand?

I'm going to be monster meat. I'm doomed. I'm totally doomed."

"My mom is calling me," Lissa whispered. "I'm not supposed to be on the phone. Bye." She clicked off.

Big help.

I stood staring at the travel bag. It was really happening. I had no choice. I had to go down there and stay with him.

As I slowly started to shove some clothes into the bag, I had only one question in my mind: *How long will I survive?*

26

Monroe's parents seemed nice. They are both short and kind of chubby. They both have straight black hair and round pink faces. Mr. Morton has a square black mustache that looks like a paint-brush. He wears thick, round eyeglasses that make his eyes appear to bulge.

He looks kind of like a bullfrog with a mustache.

Marni and Mickey are Monroe's sister and brother. Marni is six and Mickey is seven, and they are both total pests. As soon as I sat down on the couch in the living room, they both started to climb on me. Like I was a playground or something.

"Don't pay any attention to them," Mr. Morton said. "They fight all the time and wrestle and scrap."

"Yes," Mrs. Morton chimed in, "they're little monsters."

Uh-oh.

Monroe was very quiet around his family. Maybe because his brother and sister were so noisy.

The bedrooms were off to one side of the apartment. Monroe's room was at the very back. It was small, about the same size as mine.

I saw bunk beds against the far wall. He had a small desk and a laptop, a low dresser, and a green leather chair with a tear down one arm.

"You need some posters on the walls or something," I said. "These bare gray walls . . ."

"It looks like a prison cell," he said. "You're right. But we just moved in. A lot of stuff hasn't been unpacked yet. Like my sports posters."

I was trying desperately to act normal. I kept thinking I could just take off. Run away. Stay in the woods for a week. But, of course, I couldn't.

I could hear Marni and Mickey arguing about something down the hall. Monroe and I worked on our math homework side by side at his small desk.

I kept glancing around the room, looking for clues. But there was nothing to see. His room really *was* as bare as a prison cell.

It was late when we finished. He motioned to the bunk beds. "Which one do you want? Top or bottom?"

I couldn't decide. I'd never slept in a bunk bed. "Which one do you usually sleep in?" I asked.

He pointed to the bottom. "I toss and turn and roll around a lot at night," he said. "So I sleep in the bottom bunk."

"Okay," I said. "I'll take the top."

Will I be safer in the top bed? Will it be harder for him to reach me if he turns into a monster?

We changed into pajamas. I climbed to the top and got settled in the bed. Monroe clicked off the light and climbed into his bed.

"This is cool," he said.

"Totally cool," I lied. I had my phone hidden under my pillow. In case I had to call someone for help. I pulled the covers up to my chin.

I suddenly thought about my nightmare. Would I have my monster nightmare tonight?

I was *living* the nightmare. Why should I dream it?

Beneath me, I heard Monroe roll over. He groaned.

Maybe I should try to stay up all night, I told myself. *Stay alert in case he attacks.*

But all the stress had made me tired. I yawned. My eyelids felt heavy. I shut my eyes and drifted into a deep, dreamless sleep.

Sometime later, a noise made me wake up. I sat up and banged my head on the ceiling.

"Oww." It took me a few seconds to remember where I was. I reached for my phone to check the time. Two thirty in the morning.

"Monroe?" I whispered. I leaned over the side of the mattress and peered through the heavy darkness down to Monroe's bed.

Empty.

He wasn't there.

I heard a fluttering sound. The window curtains flying into the room. I turned and stared. The bedroom window was wide open. Nothing but darkness on the other side.

My heart started to thud in my chest. The breeze from the open window chilled me.

Monroe was gone. The window was open. He must have sneaked out. Sneaked out at two thirty in the morning.

Did the monster go out to prowl?

I grabbed my phone and swung myself down to the floor. I changed back into my clothes as quickly as I could pull them on.

I knew what I had to do. I had to follow him.

27

I swung one leg over the window ledge and stepped out onto the pavement. I could feel the darkness sweep over me like a blanket. There was no moon. No light here at the back of the apartment building.

I took a deep breath, sucking in the cold night air. I waited for my eyes to adjust to the darkness. But I could see only shades of gray and black.

I took a step away from the building. Then another.

I froze when I saw something move to my right. A figure, black against the black wall. Yes. Someone moving rapidly away from the building.

I forced my legs to move and started after it. It was lumbering heavily, moving toward the street.

I stayed back. I tried to move as silently as I could.

111

It turned suddenly, into an alley that ran behind a row of small houses. I knew the alley. Sometimes Lissa and I use it as a shortcut home from school.

I ignored the chills running down my body and followed silently. The lumbering figure knocked over a metal trash can, and the lid banged noisily as it rolled away.

I stepped into a patch of soft mud. I clapped my hand over my mouth to stop my cry of surprise.

And then pale light seeped down as a tiny sliver of a moon poked out from behind heavy clouds. And in the dim light, I saw it.

Saw the monster.

Yes. A fur-covered beast. Big and wide. Banging through the alley, bumping against fences, knocking trash cans on their sides.

I could see it clearly. Proof. Proof that Monroe is a monster, a monster out on its nightly prowl.

I stopped and pulled the phone from my pocket. I raised it close and made sure the flash was turned off. Then I clicked a photo of the creature. Then another and another.

I took a step closer. Then I pulled back as the creature suddenly bent down.

It grabbed at something. I squinted into the misty light. Squinted hard. And saw the dead rabbit in its paws. Yes. It grabbed a dead rabbit and pulled it to its mouth.

And began to *eat*.

Monroe the monster was feasting on a dead rabbit.

My body trembled with the horror of what I was seeing. And I couldn't help it. I let out a moan. "Ohhhh."

The monster dropped the rabbit corpse and spun quickly. Spun to face me.

"Nooo!" I cried.

I stumbled. I landed on my knees in the dirt.

It moved so fast. It pounced. It pressed me to the ground. Pushed me hard into the dirt. And whispered: *"I told you. You're NEXT!"*

28

It pressed its knee into my back, holding me down. It weighed a ton. I struggled to breathe.

"Please —" I choked out.

I could hear it grunting, breathing hard.

"Please — let me up," I begged.

"*I warned you*," it snarled. It lifted its knee. The big creature climbed to its feet. It grabbed me by the arms and hoisted me up.

"Let me go. . . ." I whispered.

It backed me against the alley fence. It pushed me hard against the rough wood planks.

"*I warned you.*"

I raised both arms in front of me, like a shield. But I knew there was no way I could defend myself.

It stood over me, eyes blazing, big stomach heaving up and down as it panted. Its hot breath brushed my face and made my skin burn.

"Monroe — please," I said in a trembling voice.

"Please. I'm your friend. We're good friends — right?"

It stared at me with deep red eyes and didn't reply.

"Monroe, why are you doing this? Why do you want to hurt me?"

It still refused to answer. It ground its huge teeth as if preparing to bite.

"Please," I begged. "Monroe — please don't hurt me."

And then the monster tossed back its big gorilla head and burst out laughing. A roaring laugh that shook the trees all around.

Tears of laughter poured from its eyes. Its whole body quivered. The sound of the booming laugh echoed down the dark, empty alley.

And as I stared, confused, trembling in fear, the monster began to change.

The thick fur stood straight up on end. Then it appeared to slide into the creature's skin. In seconds, the fur vanished and I could see pale skin.

The monster began to shrink. Its wide body pulled in, became slender, and it grew shorter . . . shorter . . . until it was about my height.

Its shoulders pulled back. Its arms grew shorter.

With the fur gone, I could see that it was wearing clothes. Human clothes. Jeans and a dark top.

It had its head down. Long hair covered its face.

Slowly ... slowly ... it raised its head. It raised its face to me. The pale moonlight washed over it. I could see its face so clearly.

Trembling in fear, unable to breathe, I stared. Stared at the human in front of me.

And finally, I choked out, "LISSA! It's *you*! Lissa!"

29

She brushed back her hair with both hands. She straightened her black T-shirt.

"It was you all along," I said. "Lissa, *you* are the monster!"

A strange smile spread over her face. She nodded slowly.

"I-I've been accusing the wrong person," I stammered. I pressed my back against the fence, struggling to stop the shudders that ran down my body.

"It was you," I said, "in the hamburger restaurant, at the pet store, in the swimming pool."

She nodded again. A cool gust of wind fluttered her hair. A cat cried somewhere in the distance.

"And I left the dead gerbil in your room, Bean. I told your dad I had to leave some homework for you. And I left it in your room."

"But ... but ..." I sputtered. "Why? Tell me. Why?"

She gazed hard into my eyes. "I had to scare you," she said finally, in a soft whisper.

"Huh? Scare me? Why?"

"To help you."

It was my turn to laugh. A hoarse snicker escaped my throat. "You scared me to help me? That's crazy!" I screamed. "*You* are my monster problem, Lissa! You weren't trying to help me. You were trying to *terrify* me!"

"Listen to me, Bean —" She tried to hold me against the fence. But I slid out of her grasp.

"Do you think I'm an *idiot*?" I cried. "You're a monster. And all you wanted to do is *terrify* me."

I didn't give her a chance to say anything else. I swung away from her and took off running. My shoes thudded the ground. I had to get away, to get back to the safety of Monroe's apartment.

Running hard, I glanced behind me. Lissa wasn't following me. But her shout rang in my ears:

"I'm warning you — don't tell anyone!"

I didn't answer. I lowered my shoulders and ran.

"Don't tell anyone!" Lissa screamed again. "Friends don't tell on friends!"

Friends?

"Friends don't *terrify* friends," I muttered. "Friends don't turn into monsters."

I didn't slow down till I ran into the deep shadow of our apartment building. Gasping for breath, I spotted Monroe's bedroom window along the back.

I grabbed the ledge and hoisted myself into the apartment.

The bedroom light was on. Monroe sat on the edge of his bed.

He looked up as I burst into the room. "Where were you?" he asked, narrowing his eyes at me.

"I — I thought you went out," I said, struggling to catch my breath. "I saw the open window. I . . . I followed you."

Monroe shook his head. He tugged down a sleeve of his pajama shirt. "I didn't go out, Bean," he said softly. "I went to the kitchen for a glass of water. When I came back, you were gone."

My legs were trembling from my long run. I dropped to the floor. "I . . . I'm sorry," I stammered. "I had it all wrong. Everything. I had everything wrong."

I saw his water glass on the desk. I grabbed it and drank it down.

"What are you talking about?" Monroe asked. "What were you *doing* out there?"

I held my breath. *Should I tell him about Lissa? Should I?*

I *had* to tell him. I had to tell someone. I had to make *someone* believe that I wasn't going crazy.

Monroe could help me, I decided. He was my friend. He could help tell my parents. He could help keep me safe from Lissa.

I told him everything. How I followed the monster down the alley. How I snapped photos with my camera. How the monster changed into Lissa.

When I finished talking, I was breathing hard. I stared at Monroe, waiting for him to react.

To my surprise, he started to laugh.

"No, Monroe," I said. "It isn't funny. It isn't a joke. Here. Let me show you. I have proof."

I grabbed my phone. I brought up my photos. My hand trembled as I flipped through them. "I have proof. Right here."

No. I didn't have proof. "Oh, nooo," I groaned. The photos were solid black.

Monroe laughed harder.

"Stop it!" I begged. "Please — stop laughing. The monster is real. Listen to me. You've got to believe me. Lissa is a monster!"

That made him totally lose it. He laughed so hard, he started to choke. That made him laugh even harder. He laughed till tears ran down his cheeks.

I couldn't stop myself. I grabbed him by both shoulders and shook him. "Monroe — stop. It isn't funny. Why are you laughing?"

His smile faded. To my surprise, he leaned forward. He brought his mouth close to my ear. And he whispered: "Bean, friends don't tell on friends."

I gasped. I let go of him and stumbled back. *What did he mean by that?*

30

How did I sleep that night?

I didn't. I thought I might never sleep again. Lissa was the monster. Lissa was the one who had pointed at me and said, *"You're next."*

Monroe slept soundly in the bunk under me. He didn't seem to care about any of my problems. For some reason, he thought it was all a joke.

Trust me. It was not a joke.

Did I feel like going to school for the pet fair the next day?

Three guesses.

But I had no choice. Every sound made me jump. Every loud voice made me want to scream and hide. But I had to pretend everything was normal.

Until I could get help . . . from someone.

I brought two red-and-purple fighting fish to the gym for the pet fair. I set up a big glass aquarium on a table near the front, filled it with water, dropped the mean little fish in, and let them do their thing.

The gym echoed with the sounds of kids setting up their pet displays. I turned when I heard screams and wild laughter. I saw that Justin Bradshaw's monkey had escaped and was climbing the exercise rope to the ceiling.

That started three or four dogs barking. They all began pulling on their leashes, desperate to chase after the monkey. The monkey reached the top of the rope easily. Then it looked down, and I *swear* it waved to all of us down below.

Coach Waller appeared and asked for volunteers to climb the rope and bring down the monkey. When no one volunteered, the big dude did it himself. Everyone cheered when he handed the monkey back to Justin.

The pet fair was off to a great start.

Four teachers had been chosen as judges. They would move from pet to pet. And the kids would each give a short talk about their pet.

But the judging wasn't scheduled until eleven o'clock. I was on the committee to watch over the pets while everyone went to class.

A big responsibility. The gym emptied out, and there I was — in charge of the monkey and the dogs that wanted to get the monkey, and the cats and lizards and ferrets, and all the other pets.

Two other kids were supposed to share the pet-watch job. But so far, they hadn't shown up.

So here I was all alone in the big gym with all the animals.

I decided to phone the office and find out where the other two kids were. But I didn't get a chance, because the monster broke into the gym.

The big, furry beast came charging across the floor, grunting and growling.

"Lissa! Get *out* of here!" I screeched. "What are you *doing* here?"

Her big, furry feet thudded heavily on the gym floor as she ran up to my aquarium on the front table.

"Lissa — nooooo!" My scream echoed off the tile gym walls.

She lifted the glass aquarium in both hands. Raised it over her head and tilted it. The water came rushing out onto the floor. Then she tilted the glass over her face — and caught the two fish in her open mouth as they came falling out.

She swallowed them with a loud *glumpf*.

"Lissa — please! Get *out* of here!" I shrieked.

She ignored me and *heaved* the empty aquarium against the wall. The glass shattered into a million pieces.

"Lissa —" I froze in horror. How could I stop her?

She opened a wire cage and let two white rats escape and go scrambling across the floor. Then she knocked over three or four cages on the next table. She pulled the monkey from its cage and sent it scampering toward the open door.

"Lissa — why?" I screamed. "Why? Why are you doing this?"

She tipped a table over and two ferret cages came crashing to the floor.

Finally, she turned to me. She pointed a furry paw and waved it at me. *"Friends don't tell on friends!"* she growled.

Then she opened the door to a parrot cage. Pulled the bird from its perch and sent it hopping clumsily across the floor.

"Lissa — please stop! I won't tell. I promise. I won't tell."

She spun away and went roaring from the gym.

Ferrets darted back and forth over my feet. The parrot was flapping its wings frantically, trying to get up to the high gym window. The monkey was chattering like a maniac, chasing after a terrified rabbit.

I struggled to catch my breath. I could feel the blood pulsing at my temples. I grabbed the wall to steady myself.

I heard footsteps. I turned and saw Mrs. Fielding walk into the gym. Her eyes bulged and her mouth dropped open in horror.

"Noah?" She kept blinking and shaking her head as she stared at the tables on their sides, the broken glass, the creatures running free all over the gym.

She gazed all around. Her eyes landed on me. Of course, I was the only one in the gym.

"Noah?" she cried. "What have you done? You'd better come with me. Why did you do this? Why, Noah? Are you *crazy*?"

31

Mrs. Fielding pulled me to her classroom. She slid a chair up beside her desk and motioned for me to sit down.

I knew I was in major trouble. Could I explain my way out of it? How could I ever explain? My hands were suddenly sweaty and left wet fingerprints on the arms of the chair.

Mrs. Fielding leaned across the desk with her hands folded on the desktop in front of her. "I'm trying to stay calm," she said. "But I am shocked and horrified. I can't understand why you went berserk in the gym. You've never done anything bad the whole time you've been at this school."

She waited for me to say something. But my brain was spinning. I just sat and stared at her.

She reached for the phone on the desk. "I'm sorry. I have to call your parents, Noah."

"Y-you can't," I stuttered. "They're away."

She squinted at me. "Well, who are you staying with?"

"Monroe's parents. But — but . . . let me explain, Mrs. Fielding."

Yes. I decided to explain. I decided to tell her everything. I didn't want to be thrown out of school for something I didn't do. Why should my whole life be ruined when it wasn't my fault at all?

"Listen to me, Mrs. Fielding," I said, leaning over the desk. "Please believe me. You know me, right? You know I'm not a troublemaker. It was Lissa. Lissa is a monster. She broke into the gym and wrecked everything. I couldn't do anything about it. She's a *monster*. Really. And I —"

I heard a cough behind me. I turned to the office door — and saw Lissa watching from the hallway. Watching and listening.

She was growling under her breath. Her face was locked in an angry scowl. Her eyes were on me. She looked ready to *kill*.

32

"I'll talk to Lissa," Mrs. Fielding said. "But I have no choice, Noah. I have to suspend you. I have to send you home. And you need to have your parents call me as soon as you hear from them."

"But, Mrs. Fielding —"

"This is serious, Noah. Very, very serious." She stood up. "Here. Come with me. Before you go home, I want you to help with the cleanup in the gym."

So that's what happened. I helped the janitor and his staff round up all the escaped pets. Then I helped clean up the incredible mess.

It was late afternoon by the time the job was finished. The school had emptied out. I packed up my backpack and headed for home.

My brain was totally messed up. I felt as if my head was going to explode.

I knew I was doomed. I had squealed on Lissa — and she saw me do it.

I kept glancing all around. I knew she'd come after me now. And I was right.

I was a block from home when I felt strong hands grab my shoulders from behind. I turned with a gasp — and saw Lissa. Lissa the monster, covered in fur. Her mouth hung open to reveal her yellow, pointed teeth.

"Bean." She growled my name angrily. "Bean — you told on me. You should never tell on a friend."

"I . . . I had no choice," I said.

"Friends don't tell on friends!" she repeated in a fierce animal roar. She grabbed my shoulders again and squeezed hard. Pain rushed down my body. Her eyes bulged wide with anger.

"I'm giving you a five-minute head start," she rumbled. "Then I'm coming after you."

"Wh-what are you going to do to me?" I stammered.

"I'll give you a hint," she growled. "You won't be *you* when I'm finished."

"Ohhhh." A frightened moan escaped my throat.

I swung away from her. For a long moment, I froze, froze in total panic. Then I forced my legs to move — and I took off.

33

But where could I hide?

Would I be safe at Monroe's apartment? Could he hide me somewhere and tell Lissa I wasn't there?

Maybe one of his parents was home. Maybe they could protect me from Lissa, the angry monster.

Ignoring a sharp pain in my side, I ran full-speed to our apartment building. I glanced back again — and saw the monster racing after me.

She lied. She didn't give me a five-minute head start.

Of COURSE she lied. She's a monster. She's been lying to me all along.

I had to outrun her. I had to get to the safety of Monroe's apartment.

Please — somebody be home, I prayed to myself.

The monster came roaring closer. Her thundering footsteps boomed in my ears, so loud I couldn't think.

Up ahead, I saw the front doors to the apartment building. But I turned away from them and ran along the side of the building. By the time I reached the back, I was gasping for breath and my chest felt about to burst.

Monroe's bedroom window was open. I grabbed the window ledge and hoisted myself inside. Then I turned and slammed the window shut.

"Anyone home?" My voice came out in a breathless whisper. I grabbed my side and struggled to breathe normally.

"Anyone home?"

I found Monroe in the kitchen. He was at the counter with a tall stack of Oreos in front of him. "Bean? What's up?" he asked. "You came in through the window?" He had a smear of chocolate on one cheek.

"Hide me. Hide me," I choked out. "She's after me. Help me, Monroe. I need your help."

He stared at me, chewing on a cookie.

"Don't just sit there," I cried. "Where can I hide from her? Where?"

"You can't," he said. He climbed down from the kitchen stool. "You can't hide from her, Bean."

"Why? What are you saying?" I demanded. "What do you mean?"

"You . . . can't . . . hide . . ." he repeated. His voice changed. It became low and gruff.

And then Monroe began to change. Brown fur

sprouted over his face. Quickly, the fur covered his neck. I saw it sprout darkly over his arms.

His eyes bulged and glowed red. His shoulders spread. He appeared to grow taller and wider. Large yellow teeth poked from his mouth. He grunted as he breathed.

"No!" I cried, backing to the wall. "No! You, too, Monroe! You're a monster, too!"

He opened his mouth in an ugly growl.

I heard a banging on the apartment door. Three loud bangs, hard enough to shake the door.

Monroe spun around and lumbered to the door. He pulled it open and Lissa burst in.

I stared at the two monsters. Two monsters who had their red eyes locked on me. Two monsters moving in for the kill.

34

I hunched against the wall, curling my body into a tight ball.

I shut my eyes and waited for them to attack.

Silence. The only sound was their grunting breaths.

I opened my eyes. They both stood at the kitchen counter, side by side, watching me.

"I ... I can't believe you're both monsters," I choked out.

Lissa rolled her red eyes. "Don't you get it, Bean? Don't you finally get it?"

"Where do we live?" Monroe snarled. "What's the name of this apartment house?"

"Huh?" I gaped at them. "It's Sternom House."

"Well, rearrange the letters in Sternom," Lissa rasped. "What do they spell?"

"*Monster!*" Monroe said. "Monster House."

My mouth was hanging open. My brain was spinning. "You mean ... this is a building for *monsters?*"

"Duh," Monroe said. "You're catching on."

"Y-you mean —?" I was too stunned to speak. "My parents?"

"Monsters," Monroe growled. "Everyone in this building. It's a monster building, Bean."

"My parents knew all along? Why didn't they tell me?"

"Not allowed," Lissa rasped. "Everyone has to find his own monster. It's inside you, Bean. Your monster is inside you, waiting to come out. But you've been fighting it."

"That's why Lissa has been scaring you," Monroe said. "She's been trying to *scare* your monster out. To make you realize who you really are."

"I told you we've been trying to help you," Lissa said. "Help you solve your monster problem."

Monroe lifted a brown bottle off the counter, stomped over to me, and shoved it into my face. "Drink this. Now."

I tried to push it away. "What is it?"

"It's Monster Helper," Monroe said. "It's just water with a little bit of monster added. You're almost there. This will do the trick. You'll see."

"No way," I said. "No way."

He pushed the bottle in my face. "Drink it. Hurry, Bean."

Lissa moved quickly. She grabbed my arms in her furry paws and pinned them behind my back.

"Please," I begged. "Please don't make me drink this stuff."

I tried to squirm and twist my head away. But Lissa held me tight. I was helpless.

Monroe tilted the bottle into my mouth and poured the cold liquid down my throat. He emptied the bottle, then tossed it to the floor.

Lissa let go of my arms.

I stood there, tasting the thick liquid on my tongue. Kind of sour ... a little like tomato juice ...

They stood watching me in silence.

Then they appeared to go fuzzy. And shake. No. The whole room was shaking. All a blur. All a trembling blur.

I felt so weird ... so totally weird.

What was *happening* to me? What did they *do* to me?

35

The woods smelled leafy fresh. I took a deep sniff of the rich, tangy dirt, the mossy tree trunks, the fragrant weeds. Then I tossed my head back and howled at the clear blue sky.

Monroe and Lissa were at my sides as we went crashing through the bushes and tall weeds. The cool wind felt so nice against my fur. My heavy paws trod lightly on the carpet of crunchy dead leaves as we trotted together.

I spotted a beehive on a low tree branch. I swiped it off the tree in both paws. Then I raised it to my snout and sucked the honey out of it.

Bees swarmed angrily as I drank my fill and passed the hive to my friends. I swatted the bees away without a worry. Then we all raised our faces to the sun and roared together.

That's how my story ends. A happy ending. No more nightmares.

You see, with my friends' help, I finally solved my monster problem. I discovered my true self.

With their help, I finally realized who the monster in my dreams was. It was ME!

And now, I'm so happy I found myself. The real me. I met my monster — and it's ME!

As we trotted through the woods, enjoying every color, every smell, Monroe poked me in the side. "Hey," he growled, "let's go to Harlan's house and have some fun with him."

Such an awesome idea. All three of us laughed and howled.

We roared and howled all the way to the poor guy's house.

Goosebumps®
MOST WANTED

Turn the page for a peek at another all-terrifying thrill ride from R.L. Stone.

I know I'm supposed to be careful. I know I'm supposed to be good. But sometimes you have to take a chance and hope no one is watching.

Otherwise, life would be totally boring, right?

My name is Jay Gardener. I'm twelve and sometimes I can't help it — I like a little excitement. I mean, dare me to do something — and it's done.

It's just the way I am. I'm not a bad dude. Sure, I'm in trouble a lot. I've been in some pretty bad trouble. But that doesn't mean I'm a criminal or anything.

Check out these big blue eyes. Are these the eyes of a criminal? No way. And my curly red hair? And the freckles on my nose? You might almost call me *cute*, right?

Okay, okay. Let's not get sickening about it.

My sister, Kayla, calls me Jay Bird because she says I'm as cute as a bird. Kayla is totally weird. Besides, she has the same red hair and blue eyes. So why pick on *me*?

So, okay, I felt this temptation come on. You know what that is. Just a strong feeling that you have to do something you maybe shouldn't do.

I gazed up and down our street. No one around. *Good.* No one to watch me.

The summer trees' leaves shimmered in the warm sunlight. The houses and lawns gleamed so bright, I had to squint. I stepped into the shade of Mr. McClatchy's front yard.

McClatchy lives in the big old house across the street from us. He's a mean dude and everyone hates him. He's bald and red-faced and as skinny as a toothpick. He wears his pants way up high so the belt is almost up to his armpits.

He yells at everyone in his high, shrill voice. He's always chasing kids off his lawn — even new kids, like Kayla and me. He's even mean to our dog, the sweetest golden Lab who ever lived — Mr. Phineas.

So, I had an idea to have a little fun. Of course it was wrong. Of *course* it wasn't what I was supposed to be doing. But sometimes, when you see something funny to do — you just have to take a chance.

Am I right?

That morning, I saw some guys in green uniforms doing work on the tall trees in McClatchy's front yard. When they went home, they left a ladder leaning against a tree.

I glanced up and down the street again. Still no one in sight.

I crept up to the ladder and grabbed its sides. I slid it away from the tree trunk. The ladder was tall but light. Not hard to move.

Gripping it tightly by the sides, I dragged it to the front of McClatchy's house. I leaned it against the wall. Then I slid it to the open window on the second floor.

Breathing hard, I wiped my sweaty hands on the legs of my jeans. "Sweet," I murmured. "When McClatchy comes home, he'll see the ladder leaning up against the open window. And he'll totally panic. He'll think a burglar broke into his house."

The idea made me laugh. I have a weird laugh. It sounds more like hiccupping than laughing. Whenever I laugh, my whole family starts to laugh because my laugh is so strange.

Well, actually, Mom and Dad haven't been laughing with me much lately. Maybe I've done some things that aren't funny. Maybe I've done some things I shouldn't have. That's why I had to promise to be good and stay out of trouble.

But the ladder against the open window was definitely funny. And it wasn't such a bad thing to do, right? Especially since McClatchy is the meanest, most-hated old dude in the neighborhood.

Still laughing about my joke, I turned and started down the driveway. McClatchy has a tall hedge along the bottom of his yard. It's like a wall. I guess he really wants to keep people out.

At the end of the driveway, his mailbox stood on a tilted pole. And as I passed it, I saw the trash cans in the street. The trash was bulging up under the lids — and it gave me another cool idea.

Working fast, I pulled open the mailbox, lifted the lid off a trash can — and started to stuff trash into McClatchy's mailbox.

Yes! A greasy bag of chicken bones. A crushed soup can. Some gooey yellow stuff that looked like puke. Wet newspapers. More soup cans.

I imagined McClatchy squeaking and squealing in his high voice when he opened the mailbox and found it jammed with disgusting garbage.

What a hoot.

I started to laugh again — but quickly stopped. A choking sound escaped my throat.

Whoa.

Someone watching me. *Two* people watching, half-hidden by the tall hedge.

I froze. They stood side by side, staring right at me. I knew they saw everything. *Everything.*

A chunk of moldy cheese and a clump of newspaper fell from my hands. I staggered back from the mailbox.

Caught. I was totally caught.

About the Author

R.L. Stine's books are read all over the world. So far, his books have sold more than 300 million copies, making him one of the most popular children's authors in history. Besides Goosebumps, R.L. Stine has written the teen series Fear Street and the funny series Rotten School, as well as the Mostly Ghostly series, The Nightmare Room series, and the two-book thriller *Dangerous Girls*. R.L. Stine lives in New York with his wife, Jane, and Minnie, his King Charles spaniel. You can learn more about him at www.RLStine.com.

The Original Bone-Chilling Series

The Original Bone-Chilling Series

■▲SCHOLASTIC

www.scholastic.com/goosebumps